Ásta Sigurðardóttir

NOTHING TO BE RESCUED

Translated by Meg Matich

nordisk books

Published by Nordisk Books, 2023
www.nordiskbooks.com

Copyright © the Estate of Ásta Sigurðardóttir.
Published by agreement with Forlagið, www.forlagid.is

This English translation copyright © Meg Matich, 2022.
Cover design © Nordisk Books

This book has been translated with financial support from:

 **ICELANDIC LITERATURE CENTER**

Printed by Severn in the UK

A CIP catalogue record for this book is
available from the British Library

ISBN 9781803522548

Nothing to be Rescued

Contents

For those whose stories go untold.

For Ásta.

I'm sitting at a plastic laminate table behind a glass divider, the only spot in the room with a jeweller's magnifier lamp. My back is to the archivist's desk, her guarded stacks concealed behind immaculate glass, which I imagine as shatterproof. Leave no marks here, I think.

A woman emerges carrying three crisp white boxes. I feel like a passenger riding backward on a train.

The first box holds illustrations, 8x10, with rounded edges: playing cards, hand-drawn, hand-painted in so many colours. Some suits are left unfinished—outlines of grey, incipient bodies. This is Ásta's famous folklore deck, which she did not complete.

The next contains ephemera, her personal belongings: a brochure for the church in Skálholt and its bishop's tomb, an artist book from City Lights in San Francisco (BOMB, Gregory Corso, 1958), an empty envelope addressed to the bond department of a defunct bank. A personal ad, written in rhyming verse, clipped out of the paper and latched into the gutter of a notebook (a good girl, orderly, reply c/o). A love letter to her children, written and rewritten, different attempts. Several poems or fictions— the genre isn't clear, but the intensity of her need is. They're feral scrawlings, ciphers rendered in a stupor. And this typewritten note (roughly translated):

...be like a seed that grows from the dark soil toward the sun and the day and becomes a gigantic tree that spreads its branches wide. [...] May fortune follow you. Burn this letter. My thoughts are best kept in flames.........

Twenty minutes before the archive closes, I reach the final box – and find a folder of drafts and unpublished stories (which she may have been gathering for a collection), handwritten neatly in a flowing script. "Death of the Drunkard" – its first line knocks the wind out of me. I translate it, very roughly. It's nailed to the page, a signpost at the turnoff to an impassable road:

When a drunk dies, they are alone because no relatives or friends are present. They have all forgotten them long ago.

Tidily written, so tidily written.

I photograph each page, hurried but gentle, capturing this vessel for confession, this destructive force foretold.

*

One of the most famous photographs of the woman who left these boxes behind—a photograph that perhaps more than anything transformed her into an idol—was published alongside her story "Street in the Rain". She is naked from the chest up. She's wearing cat-eye liner, eyebrows sharp, carved; her lips are dark and full. She's holding a burning cigarette. She wears a metal choker as a bevor. Her hand casts a shadow over her sternum—her gaze is turned away.

A companion image, one of several, was displayed in the window of the artist's – Jón Kaldal's – studio at Laugavegur 11. Her face is turned toward me, but her eyes don't make contact; she's looking beyond me. Her left nipple is visible (though traditionally, and even now, it's cropped out). Thrice, this window was replaced because of vandalism, furious attempts to deface her brazen beauty.

This striking woman was shaped by the elements of her childhood: fragrant heath, mire, lava field, and shore. Ásta Jóna Sigurðardóttir was born on April 1, 1930 at a farmstead called Litla-Hraun to a reluctant farmer and self-taught scholar named Sigurður Benjamín Konstantínus Jónsson and his god-fearing wife, Þóranna Guðmundsdóttir, who was a staunch Adventist and hard worker. In her early years, Ásta did not have access to schooling. The farm was not equipped with running water or electricity; neither did the family have a radio. Books and stories were the entertainments of the household, and Ásta's father's fascination with literature stoked her natural creativity and brilliance. A gifted artist and writer, steeped in the riches of myth and folklore, poetry and wild country.

At 14, she moved to Reykjavík to begin a formal education— an uncommon path for a rural girl in mid-century Iceland. She began to dress in fashionable clothes that lent her an air of glamour: the movie star in a modest milieu. Soon, she'd dye her chestnut brown hair black, paint herself in the makeup of Hollywood heroines (among friends, she later earned the nickname 'Cleopatra with 11 fingers'), and sew her own garments. She would sometimes go around in a pelt. This was also when she began to drink.

At the time, Reykjavík was a fledgling city with a population of around 38,000, which had recently borne the physical and cultural shocks of industrialization and two Allied militaries who brought their cultural norms and idols to the island. The emergence of the middle class in twentieth century Iceland enabled a pronounced demarcation between home and work, and in turn, a sharp division of gender roles – a notion of "separate spheres" previously impractical in a more seasonal, agriculture and fishing-based economy. These changes to the social fabric fuelled stigmas around sex and childbearing outside of marriage in a country that, previously, was fairly tolerant of non-marital children.

In the 1940s, women and girls' lives were policed because of a manic suspicion of their relationships with Allied soldiers. Fraternization was seen by some as wanton and treasonous, and was often negatively equated with sex work. A committee formed to, ostensibly, assess the scope of the "problem" and to remediate it. In the most extreme cases, women suspected of sleeping with soldiers – their names compiled on running lists – were forced to undergo pelvic examinations. All women and girls could be subject to surveillance, interrogation. (In 2015-2016, Parliament conducted an official inquiry into this period, with particular attention to a facility called Kleppjárnsreykir).

Ásta examines this period—called "The Situation" or "Ástandið"—in her story "Lilies" through the figure of a sick, nameless young woman who twice becomes pregnant outside of marriage, first to an American soldier and later to a "good" Icelander. She lives in a Nissen barracks hut (in Icelandic: "braggi"), purchased en masse from the military by the Icelandic government for temporary, low-cost housing. She attempts to measure up to rich and fine women, even as her callous doctor insists that "people should take better care of themselves. Those old barracks aren't any place for a child." No action she takes will wash away the sin of poverty, of becoming pregnant while poor. The author herself at times lived in a Nissen hut, and – as attested to in her letters – experienced houselessness and hunger.

After receiving her secondary school diploma, she matriculated to Teacher's College. In her second year, Ásta became pregnant; it was decided that her mother would keep the child while Ásta finished her studies, but Þóranna ultimately raised this child. I find myself wondering if this loss event was, in a distant way, the inspiration for "In Which Pram"—in which a woman obsessively searches for her non-martial infant, who was taken from her at birth, furtively peering into prams while their owners are out of sight. Ásta describes these carriages in saturated detail—wealthier couples have beautiful prams, and their children have new toys and smell of powder, while poor and single mothers use baskets, roller skates, and umbrella skeletons as construction materials; they smell of sour milk. Each shoos away the protagonist, an outsider, as they would a pest.

Later, she became pregnant with the child of another artist, who coerced her into undergoing an abortion, which was only legal under the narrowest of circumstances (her pregnancy did not fit them). This may have been the foundation for one of her early stories, "The Dream", a nightmarish narrative in which reality and dream smear across another during a young woman's unsafe abortion; after, when she is bleeding, disoriented, and stumbling, the fine people of Reykjavik jeer at the blood "puddled on the back of [her] dress."

"Harlot!" One calls, "Don't you want to change your clothes?"

*

Ásta's lifestyle and worldview exiled her from mainstream society. Work was scarce, and Ásta's housing situation was unstable. Though she struggled with poverty and house-lessness, she pursued mentorships and became part of a cohort of like-minded artists — bohemians such as the Atom Poets — who shared her values and embraced an exploration of inner life through dreamlike narratives. They frequented cafés — Hressingarskálinn, Kommakaffi, Laugavegur 11 ("Ellefu")— that were safe spaces for queer self-expression. As Bragi Kristjónsson colourfully illuminates in his 1992 article, Ellefu's regulars were "artists, scholars, students, and other successful and unsuc-cessful intellectuals, aficionados of arts and education, small-time thieves and eccentrics, editors and journalists, and half-unhinged folk."

For a time, Ásta supported herself by modelling nude, which, combined with her image and the company she kept, caused a stir. She was known to take her breaks stark naked, reminding shocked passers-by that she was 'in her work uniform'. Audacious, big, alive. Because of her appearance and mystique, she has been mythologised as the bohemian ideal. However, this obscures the depressing reality. Like the lino-cuts Ásta created to illustrate many of her stories, she is a remnant, the pattern left when shadow is cut from light. A process of constitution through subtraction.

Ásta's breakthrough came shortly after she received her teaching degree, with the story "Sunday Night to Monday Morning", the seminal work that would become the title of her 1961 collection, in the periodical *Líf og list*; at the time, literary circles praised its ingenuity and bravery, but the mainstream saw it as scandalous, shameful. "Sunday Night to Monday Morning" relates a surreal account—Ásta's—of a young woman who is assaulted while vulnerable and intoxicated. In its strange poetry, it makes tangible the sense of disembodiment one might experience during a traumatic event. As in her other stories, her naïve protagonist's worldview pendulates between an anchored belief that "people are good," and instinctual horror and fear at the deliberate harm they do.

Fittingly, the story is now lauded as a brave Me Too story—one in which I have found a tarnished mirror. With sirenic insistence, this story called. My answer is this translation.

*

Even as she blossomed in an artistic society, Ásta's alcohol dependence continued to worsen. She discarded a 300-page novel. During her partnership with the poet Þorsteinn frá

Hamri, the pair had five children. They were born in quick succession, with only six years between the youngest and the oldest. Her accelerating cycles of benders lessened her ability to care for herself and her children, and her partner soon left. After this, her children were repeatedly removed from her care. The trauma of losing them replayed on an endless loop, a circuit of shocks soldered by a disease of despair.

Ásta appears to have sought treatment several times, but toward the end of her life, the depth of her addiction had become so profound that she was willing to drink whatever was at hand, including antifreeze, to feel drunk. On December 21, 1971, at the age of 41, she died of complications of alcohol abuse.

*

In one of her final letters to her children in March of 1971, she speaks of her unwavering belief in the wonder of language and literature. She writes: "…try to learn all of the best verses by heart […] and to understand the language, to sense how Icelandic glitters like frost on a still, white day."

Ásta's work continues to thrive because of the familiarity of these stories, their symmetry with other women's experiences of shame, neglect, harm—and of power, resilience, care. They are the stories of those whose stories go untold. She approaches these subjects with, in the poet Sjón's words, "restrained anger and compassion for those [she] had broken bread with on her own turbulent journey".

And they are flashes of clarity. In them are moments where I can see Ásta's mind playing out and processing trauma from a safe distance, critiquing a society that banished those who didn't follow its templated paths – that laughed at a bleeding woman.

I selected the title of this slim volume, *Nothing to be Rescued*, rather than the name of Ásta's best-known story and the title of her 1961 collection, because of the phrase's interpretive possibilities. It is, to me, the meeting point of self-assertion and self-erasure: where love and fear collide.

These stories, ten of many, hold powerful warnings. In Ásta's frissonic prose, they are living wonders, too.

AN ANIMAL STORY

…and then the big, big animal runs and runs, chasing the little animal, harder and harder, but it isn't scared and it isn't tired like the little animal because the game is such great fun. It's like a cat tormenting a little mouse before killing it. It's such great, great fun!

The man paused to catch his breath. He'd gotten himself excited. It was even better than the cinema. There, it's dark and you can only hear the audience's horror, but in this child's pale and gaunt face, he could read the terror. Her grubby little hands gripped her armrest like a vice and she sat pigeon-toed, her feet glued to the polished floor. She looked like an animal that's scared half to death.

He admired his own creative genius, his ability to play so with the child's imagination. Of course, scaring a six, seven year-old child is no great feat, you could argue. After all, she was small for her age and immature; anybody could manage it. But that wasn't the case here.

When normal people spook children with stories, it's generally short-lived. The kids forget it soon after. It might scare them the first time, but its power diminishes with each telling. The story loses its effect and becomes every-day, nothing more than a harmless joke; few have the capacity to give the story a bad ending time after time. And no child is so dim as to believe a story that ends one way today, and the opposite the next. At most, kids will believe what they see fit.

But this story was a different beast altogether. He felt that he was a genius. And he could back up his story merely by pointing to the picture. Pictures never lie.

He could see the child's fear and antipathy taking root. The girl was having trouble falling asleep in the evening, and she slept only intermittently. She stared at other children out to play and said nothing. At the dinner table, she absentmindedly nibbled at her food. He watched her grow thinner day by day.

At first, she had poured over the picture, staring at these two unlike animals until she got tired. When she moved her lips, he knew that she was recalling the story, the dreadful words he had put in her mouth. She certainly didn't understand them all, but she knew they meant something terrible. And that was enough. He knew, too, what went on in her little head, under her thin, drab hair, behind her sombre, grey-blue eyes.

The child's messy half-formed thoughts obsessively circled the white animal's horrific fate. At first, she hoped the creature would get through it. She stretched out her hand and covered the little animal with her palm.

– Will it let it go? She lisped. The sweet little animal will get to its burrow, won't it? Say yes, stepdad.

He stared at her for a moment before giving his answer. Hope shined in her innocent, simpleton eyes. How he hated the remarkable strength of this powerless little creature. She was insignificant, yet she could make his wife defy him!

Imagine. His wife, Sigga, that cowardly, stupid wretch, had time and again fought him tooth and nail over the child. Sure, the weakling didn't shrink under his blows, but she winced under those he gave the disgraceful child. A thing like that.

He had often become so enraged that he wanted more than anything to squeeze the living daylights out of the girl. But that was too dangerous a method of disposing of her. That was against the law. What was not against the law was telling children stories about animals and showing them pictures.

He looked attentively at the child before dropping one simple word:

– No.

He had never so enjoyed saying a word, having the last word, or winning an argument as much as he enjoyed dropping this one 'no' and watching its effect.

The hope in her eyes burned out, and her lips began to tremble. Then she grimaced and slapped her small, grubby right hand on top of her left to protect the little animal.

– No, he repeated. Slowly and calmly, he pried her hands away from the picture and shoved her away, with all the grand superiority of the fittest. Then he grabbed the book and dangled the picture in front of the child's eyes.

– No, the poor little animal isn't spared. The big, big animal chases it for a long time. It chases it for sport. The big animal isn't tired in the least, and could go on chasing it, harder and harder, if it wanted, but it's all just for the enjoyment of scaring the little animal and wearing it out. The little animal is so terrified—so very terrified of the big animal—that it runs much harder than it can. But no matter how fast it runs, there's no hope of escape. The big animal paws at it with its long, sharp claws at its leisure. The little animal gets more and more tired. Its blood thickens and blackens in its veins out of deathly terror. Its blood turns to poison and its veins burn like a flaming fuse. When it can't run any farther, it plunges into the ground and rolls and rolls and rolls.

Ha-ha-ha! It's such a pathetic weakling— such a yellow-bellied layabout. But the bigger, stronger animal doesn't want to kill it right away. It slices a little hole in its stomach so that its intestines spill out along with some of its guts. The little animal is in such agonizing pain that it drags itself with its little wimpy, softy paws and limps forward and the big animal slows down to laugh, letting it put a little distance between them. Because it's all so laughable. Oh, yes. Ha-ha-ha-ha-ha! And the little animal tries to scramble to shelter. It wants to die right away. It hopes the big animal doesn't see it—it's just so dumb, so terrifically stupid. Ha-ha-ha-ha! It hopes that it can die in peace. But it doesn't get too far. And the big animal licks its lips, it's so clever, and it knows it. The big animal knows what's going to happen next. The little animal belly crawls with the last of its strength. But it can't see where it's going because its eyes have filled with a blood fog that clouds everything in crimson. It's so disoriented from fear and agony that it turns itself around and blunders blindly back to the big animal, and its own paws get tangled up in its own entrails and it tips over and rolls on the ground—like so.

And then it lies still, hoping death will come along and have mercy on it. It hopes that death will come soon. No. Death does not come.

But the big, big, horrible animal comes along and cuts off one of its paws, like this, and tears an even larger hole in its stomach, like this. And tears off its skin, flaying it alive with a flick of the wrist. Hah-ha! The little animal lets loose a penetrating cry. Its cries reverberate off the cliffs all around. But no one comes to help. The other animals hear its agonizing wails from a long way off. They hear them clearly and they know what they mean, but they don't help the little animal because they're also yellow, every one of them, cowering and cowardly creatures. They shrink into burrows and pray that it doesn't come for them, but it will come for them one day, every single one of them indeed, and none will be spared.

Then the big animal sheers the legs from the little animal, one after another. Its sinews are strong, but the big strong animal tears them asunder. They make an issk, issk sound as they're cut. The little animal's cries grow quieter and quieter until they turn into a rattle, a death rattle. But the little animal doesn't die until it's been completely dismembered, covered in its own blood, which oozes through the grass and ground around it.

Then it finally dies, and its agony is indescribable. The big, big animal yawns and goes off somewhere to lounge in the sun and unwind. It's not just big, this animal. It's also diligent, intelligent. When it finishes its nap, it goes to look for other little stupid animals to torment them for a bit of entertainment. And it doesn't need to search for long. There are plenty of little imbecilic creatures with big ears and big eyes that they don't use to their advantage. They're so idiotic that they let down their guard. There are plenty of animals like this. Oh yes. Plenty. And the big animal plays and naps, plays and naps. It finds more than enough mindless fools. Should I go on? Would you like that?

The girl couldn't catch her breath for her sobs. Tears brimmed in her eyes, but didn't spill over onto her cheeks. They gleamed as if frozen.

He set the book on the nightstand and stepped away with the calm strides of someone who knows they've won. That's how you do it. Tens around the board. Nobody could object.

His wife, Sigga, had tried to protest. But she was so afraid of him that she spoke to him sweetly:

– Now sweet'art, don't be filling Dísa's head with your 'orror stories, she's a del'cate one, as you well know!

He flared his nostrils with scorn and mocked her:

– Schweet'art! Look who's talking. You keep telling her stories about the crucifixion. That's no better. Telling a child about the most brutal tortures that human beings can inflict upon one another, and passing it off as the Christian story of Jesus. It's something else entirely to kill a sordid creature. And what I'm telling her is true. You should tell children the truth from the beginning.

– But Kidde, sweet'art! Dísa's gone and lost 'er appetite. And she dreams such 'orrible fings at night. And she keeps on frowin' up.

26

– But isn't that just as much your fault! It's absurd to fill kids' heads with religious nonsense and all that bullshit about Jesus before they go to bed. You just make sure you don't turn the child into a fool with your drivel.

He slammed his fists on the table to underscore his point. The woman sunk down, not daring to say more. He knew that he hadn't yet broken this abject, dull, and stupid woman, though her eyes were downcast and her movements had become jumpy. She was still certain to protect the kid; she usually shielded the girl from his blows and got in the way of his fists until he was exhausted from beating them.

He found it intolerable that he couldn't be the man of his house—and, for that matter, to be denied that right by someone as naive as Sigga. It was the worst of humiliations.

It was the kid's fault. It was as if the endurance of womankind's most wretched creatures multiplied when you laid a finger on their offspring. But now he'd pinned down a method that worked. His poor wife was defenceless against this new tactic. She couldn't tell her girl that her stepfather was telling untruths because the girl had often caught her mother out when she was lying. And she'd never caught her stepfather in a lie. On top of that, the girl didn't believe a single word of her mother's stories. Even the story of Jesus on the cross—insipid and disputable in her mother's mouth—ended inconsistently. It was nothing compared to even his least remarkable tales. Though this new story was the best one of all.

The girl couldn't think about anything else. She stared into space with her hands closed around the book. She was either afraid of the picture or knew it by heart.

And her stepfather told her the story every night, becoming ever the more grandiose in his word choice, the plot growing ever the more transfixing. The girl listened mesmerized, her mouth agape. She sniffled loudly, tears pooling in her eyes, but she held onto her cries until night-time. Then, he had a good and valid reason to get out of bed and "give her a shaking" as he called it.

The mother held her breath in fear but didn't dare move until she heard the blows resound against her child's skeletal body. Then he had to "give her a shaking", too.

It was a bit of a workout, but he saw the fruits of his labour: The woman grew ever more docile and submissive, and the child hollowed out, paled.

The book wasn't big. It was bound in red linen, which was darkened with water spots and shabby from use. It looked like it was liable to break apart in one particularly soiled and torn spot, which was visible even when the book was closed. Now, it lay on the table by the old sewing machine and the girl sat on a stool, staring at the black letters on the stained and filthy cover. They were scary symbols that she didn't understand.

– Doncha wanna look at 'em 'ere pichures o' Jesus instead? Her mother asked. She was mending the girl's almost useless coat.

The girl didn't answer.

– You know very well not to take 'em serious, her mum continued.

– No, the girl said. It's important to mind pictures.

– Yes, maybe pictures of Jesus and the like. Like 'em at 'at there Sunday school.

– And the picture of you and stepdad.

Her mother fell silent. The things kids come up with!

– It's a real picture. And the picture of the little beautiful animal is also real. And the one of the scary bad animal. It's not make-believe. But pictures of Jesus at Sunday school are make-believe. Jesus didn't need to be nailed to the cross. He could fly, he could fly up in the sky if he wanted, and get lots of angels to guard him against the bad men. But no one could help the poor little animal. That is so awful. And that was real. But Jesus didn't die on the cross except sometimes. And now he is up in heaven with lots of tasty food to eat with the angels. And there's no pain. It's just make-believe.

– God will you listen to yersel' child! You better not be talkin' that there nonsense at Sunday school!

The mother stood up and slapped her thigh in consternation. And then she went into the living room to look for patches in the dresser.

The girl stared absentmindedly at the old scissors. A moment passed before she came to her senses. She had always been forbidden to hold scissors, and even though she'd snuck them once or twice to try them out. She knew very well what they could do.

She snatched the scissors and opened the book. That awful image appeared before her. Without hesitation, the girl sliced across the pages' margins and up into the pictures to clip out the little white animal. After, only a gaping oval-shaped hole remained. She gave herself time to snip at the big scary animal and rip its head and front legs off.

The image's magical powers depleted. It was almost comical in its worthlessness. An entire tormented, horrifying world left in ruins, leaving only a mundane and peaceful nothing.

The girl slammed the book shut and put the scissors back in their place. She had time to slip the image of the little white animal into her sock before her mother returned. She stopped at the open window and let the head and forelegs of the bad animal tumble out. The wind took the scraps and swept them into the gutter.

The girl felt the world's expression lift. All that was bad, vicious, abominable was gone in an instant, but all that was good, beautiful, and gentle shone in her eyes wherever she looked. In her thoughts, she saw myriad little white faces with long, soft ears and big, innocent, dark eyes gazing at her without the least fear.

She had saved them all. The big, scary animal had disappeared into the gutter. It couldn't hurt them anymore.

Her stepfather's voice boomed and the house shook.

– Where's the rest of the picture?

This big powerful man held the child in the air and shook her like a rag. Her tattered clothes choked her soft neck and she couldn't force a sound to come out of her throat. Her little pale face was purple and swollen.

The mother could only catch glimpses from the corner of the kitchen, where she cowered knee-to-chest, pressed up against the stove. But she was so petrified she couldn't move. She couldn't so much as open her lips to pray to god and Jesus, but the voice inside of her called feverishly out to them. God—to be so powerless!

– Goddamn bloody fucking sabotaging bitch! He screamed. He held the child in the air with his left hand and used his right to strike her, to pull her hair. Then he threw her to the floor and kicked her. Something in the girl rattled, but she didn't make a sound. He was so out of his mind with rage and hatred that he couldn't stop himself. He was getting ready to lay into the girl again when the woman charged at him, spitting out wails.

He dropped his hands. He hadn't counted on this woman having the power to attack him again. He got his bearings and struck her again and again, her face, her head. Then she lost her grip on his hair and folded down to the floor.

Then he snapped out of it. He was suddenly petrified. Had he killed them?

He peered at the girl's face, which was covered in blood. No, she wasn't dead because she was whimpering violently. She moved. She even tried to crawl away. No, she was a little injured but she wasn't dead. He felt relieved.

– Now are you going to tell me where it is? He heard himself ask. He didn't know his own voice. It lacked all dignity. It was a pointless, unplanned question about something that made no difference. Not as things were now.

He had lost. That was the only thing that mattered. He had lost to this powerless and insignificant adversary.

He read his defeat in the girl's tear-soaked and blood-encrusted face, in her swollen, shut lips, in her blood-shot eyes that stared up at him. It was as if they were telling him: You can kill me. I'll never tell.

The defeat tolled in his ears in the rattle of guttural sobs coming from the woman in a pile on the floor. After many years of beatings and intimidation, this insignificant, frightened, long-suffering creature tried to intervene for her young, incited by a blind impulse that can never be dispatched.

– I'll give you both a shaking when I get back, he touted in a low voice. He felt how the threat had lost its power, so he added: I'll get myself some firewater and kill you both. That's what I'll do.

Then he walked out, slamming the door behind him.

When the woman saw the child stumble to her feet, she began to shriek wails. In between sobs, she begged god and Jesus to help her. Her lamentations stranded in the house's indifferent walls. She had no energy to stand, and so she lay where she'd landed.

The girl could hardly catch her breath for sobs. She clung instinctively to the rags wrapped around her and tried to hold the tatters together. Her little exhausted child hands shook so violently that she couldn't turn her pockets right-side out. Her stepfather had flipped them inside-out, and their poor contents lay on the floor: a piece of string in the colours of the flag; two red buttons; one golden snap; and a folded paper doll that had been clipped from the back of an oatmeal box.

The girl shuffled her feet in place, sobbing among her belongings, but made no attempt to collect them. A moment passed before she recovered her senses and remembered the little white animal.

She sat down on the floor and removed her shoes and socks. She wasn't sure which sock the picture was in, so she searched both. Yes, there, rustling in one of them, there it was. The girl gripped it and pressed it close to her carefully and kindly. To her mind, it wasn't merely a picture, but a little white animal, wonderful, beautiful, and good.

She scrambled to her feet and hurried barefoot into the bedroom. There, the table lamps' faint light illuminated the faces of her mother and her stepfather, smiling vacuously, unnaturally, in the dim red. The girl paid them no mind, but held the picture, which trembled in her hand, up to the lamp's red glow. There was a glare in her swollen eyes, so she rubbed them with the back of her hand to focus her vision. She tried to swallow her sobs.

Her stepfather hadn't found the animal. She still had it. And it hadn't been hurt, even though her stepfather had beaten her badly, beaten her all over. But why was it so scared? The animal was scared to death. She saw it in its eyes. Its big, dark eyes betrayed a violent agony. And it ran and ran! Something was chasing it—some formidable monster.

The girl stiffened with terror. She was stunned by the fear that shook through her abused body—she was now one with this little, terrified, preyed-upon animal.

The big, vicious monster still existed, it was in the room in this red dark; it would never be defeated, no, never.

The child crumpled up the image in her cold, sweaty palms in bewildered anguish. The little animal had no hope; it was condemned to death and would never reach its burrow.

LAMBING SEASON

The boy had stopped watching his steps when he ran through the barnyard. It was all the same where his feet landed. In any case, the cowslips with closed buds would die, even if he didn't tread on them. They'd freeze to death, every last one of them.

Pale and downtrodden, he paced the yard's sharp, hard ground. A pain shot through his nose as soon as he'd emerged into the cold. It was as if the air were saturated with poison fumes. His nostrils stung and he couldn't fight off the urge to sneeze.

He found himself leaping out of the way of large clusters of leafy plants without thinking; they were lined up in rows that looked like the hooves of a horse when it's rolled over on its back or it's being shoed. For the most part, they were still green but for the very youngest, which were turning black from frost. Here and there, golden heads peeked out among them, contrasting those with dark frost burns.

On the first frost of the season, he'd considered gathering the cowslips that hadn't yet blossomed and putting them in water in the kitchen, but then he realized how many they were—it was an unachievable goal—and they would likely die in the kitchen before they opened, anyway. The room was cold and narrow and dim. They didn't belong there.

The cold got into everything: the kitchen, the common room, the hallway, the cowshed, the sheep shed, the barn. It slipped into beds, under clothes, ran through all people and creatures, and it knew no match. Even freshly lit fires in the hearth cowered, faint and humiliated. At random, the fire shot up a weak blue lick—but that flame immediately slunk back into its hiding place among the frozen peat and collapsed in shame.

The boy thought astonishing that he'd withstood that long, cold winter—and he'd even felt at times merry of spirit and optimistic. In fact, he was almost cheerful despite the monotony of short, frigid days and long, soundless nights. They were most bleak when blizzards beat against the roof and squalls swept from the north, carding the withered thatch on the walls.

There was only one thing that could screw up his courage, revive him and enliven his spirits: The hope that winter would end, and anticipation of the coming spring, with its light, warmth, green grass, birdsong.

And now, spring had come at last—and gone. That made the cold feel much more bitter, the storms more frigid, the freeze more agonizing.

He shifted his weight from foot to foot near the patch of cowslip and, with an aching sadness, thought of their golden heads folded in their green sheaths, waiting for the thaw, for sun, for a southerly wind—it would all come to naught. The first ones had just begun to open their yellow blossoms.

The boy turned cold inside—it didn't sit well with him. He pursed his lips and spit into the wind. A bone-chilling gust whipped it back into his face. He wiped it off with the sleeve of his coat, feeling as though he were losing courage.

What kind of weather is this, then? He stamped his feet and hurtled straight through the cowslips, trampling their frost-trimmed leaves, stamping and kicking until nothing was left but a litter of battered stems and bruised blades, misshapen beds heaped high with the abused bodies of the baby cowslips.

The boy stepped back for a moment and contemplated the destruction.

What was he thinking, goofing around like this? Cowslips—not even—useless husks—and him, a full-grown man! A man who needed to tend to the sheep.

The boy walked slowly down the meadow, his back to the storm, and kicked horse clods out of his path, just as his father did. They were frozen solid and bounced playfully around him, as if it were a game. He straightened and stopped kicking. The game shouldn't even occur to him; he was no longer a child.

He lifted his face toward the sky and shaded his eyes with his hand, as he'd seen grownups do when they were forecasting the weather.

Then he remembered people only did that when the sun was high and bright, and he felt embarrassed. Just as well that nobody had seen. People teased him when he acted like a grownup.

Now there was no light in the sky to blind.

It was plain to see that winter had returned. On that first day, his father said it was nothing more than a thin film of ice on the puddles, that that was a good sign. It didn't occur to him that a cold spell was coming. He believed spring had arrived; everyone believed it, except for gran. But nobody paid her any mind, though she'd predicted a winter storm, and the prediction had come to pass. It had been like this for a week. Even though the plover had returned and had already said *pii-pii*. And the glory, the glory, though it lisped like a toddler. The whimbrel had arrived, too, and up until that point winter had dependably come to an end when it sang its long sputtering song—which the boy himself had heard out by the out peat mines.

There was no reason to take the superstition seriously, though his gran had taught him the rhyme. And, likely, none of it meant anything. People had already begun to wish each other happy summer, to smile at one another, and to enjoy themselves as though the time to mow the meadow had already arrived. The cat had started cleaning its whiskers, and the dogs went out to play with a length of braided rope. Winter didn't linger in their minds. Only gran's.

She turned in her bed and murmured and predicted— predicted the storm.

But that wasn't all. Her speech long and drawn-out, she said:

– Though my rags may rot, mark my words: It will be quite a thing if any summer comes to pass this season. Yes, you laugh, but mark my words though my feet are turning cold.

She said that. And it could very well come true, all of it.

Then there would be no summer.

The boy crawled under the barbed wire fence, and caught his jacket on the unforgiving barbs. He pulled his jacket away from the fence with a tremendous force that left the wire singing. He paused to watch its trembling vibrations, which made it look like many strings, until the sound died out in the wind. A rag of ripped fabric had caught on the barbs, and the wind tossed it about like a sail. It snapped like the whip of an officer.

The boy broke into laughter. He startled when he heard himself: His laugh sounded exactly like his father's guffawing in the barn last night. His voice echoed somewhere, hollow and scornful, just as his father's did the empty barn, and it screeched above him like the rusty nails in the rotting and sagging battens.

The boy got scared and sprinted down the field. The frozen ground cracked under each footfall, he sank in mud halfway to his ankles, and the ground's sharpened needles of ice pierced his sealskin shoes as if to pin him in place.

When he reached the mire, he slowed, shoved his hands into his pockets. It wasn't manly to make so much of nothing.

He zigzagged out onto the ice and wove between tussock mounds. Then he stomped, hard, to test its tolerance.

What a wonder that he'd ever enjoyed the ice and snow.

No, there was no fun in it—best to avoid anything of the sort. He sprung up on his toes and slammed down his heels, and the thin ice caved under the force, shooting a long crack across the sheet.

He'd crush all this bloody ice, or at least put cracks in it. Then he fell through with a splash, landing in water up to his calves.

He fumbled out of it, and leapt away from the edge, dripping wet. At least there was plenty of water in the world that wasn't frozen—and it was about time!

The boy gazed at the muck on his shoes, which were caked in iron reds and blacks. His saturated socks began to stiffen and frost. The boy gritted his teeth.

– Oh hell! He spat out.

He gasped and reached instinctively for his throat. It had happened! He'd said it aloud! And on the way to the ewes in lambing season! He'd cursed at the worst possible moment. Though he'd often heard that word, and even heard it in his thoughts when he was furious, he trembled at the thought of saying it aloud.

Now something awful would happen! He had to pray to god post haste. He folded his thin, purple hands; his pale, gaunt face filled with even greater worry as he prayed to god for mercy.

Then he skittered away, skipping from mound to mound. He tried to wipe the rust-red and blue-black muck off his shoes on the ashen grass.

On the patchy, golden edge of the sludge below the hillocks, the boy discerned some sort of dark mass. He quickly realized it was a ewe. She paced in small orbits around the same spot, and turned around and around herself like a shearling suffering circle sickness. He hastened his steps and before long recognized his Brúska, the lamb he'd been given in the autumn, and his first ewe lamb.

He had christened her Brúska—wool tuft—because she had an unusual puff of wool on her forehead, which was thought to be a sign of a strong line.

Her fleece was pink, dirty, and soaked with blood. She must've given birth! His joy hastened his steps as he called out her name.

The yearling gazed at him fearfully, and looked as though she might take off, but instead stopped still in front of him. The boy tip-toed up to her, little by little, cautious and solemn, and reached out his hands.

– Brúska! Brúska-my-girl! Sheepy sheep!

She turned about and stumbled a few steps, snorted toward the ground, let loose a miserable and strange bleat. He'd never heard her make that sound before.

And she swung her neck, fixed her position, and stamped her front hooves defensively as if she'd never seen a man before, least of all this boy who had cared for her all winter, stroked her and cuddled her when he could get a hold of her, and preferred her to all the other yearlings.

He was a little insulted by Brúska's unusual ingratitude, but he was also excited to see the lamb, elated over his new wealth.

And there it was, so strikingly small and white, almost lying in its own afterbirth in a depression that broke the wind. But it was almost lifeless. It didn't lift its head, even though Brúska had licked its birth fluids clean.

The boy reached out his hand to grasp it, but the yearling stomped and snorted at him as though he were the adversary.

44

– Why are you acting like this, Brúska? The boy asked, both surprised and sore. I'm only trying to help you with your lamb!

But Brúska didn't seem to hear him. She rubbed her snout against her offspring and bleated dark and harsh.

And what a pitiful, vile sound! It came from deep within her gut, as if she were about to vomit. And then her breath became a bellows, and she positioned herself to charge him.

The boy was really angry now, and kicked her, making her cower.

– Get out of here, you little idiot, he said, shaking his fist in front of her snout.

He picked the lamb up. It was a ewe lamb—the first— the queen of the lambs! But her little, white head slackened in his hands and her long, thin legs dangled lifelessly in the storm. The little bundle of lamb glued itself, damp and cold, to his hands, its eyes half-closed.

The boy's breaths were heavy.

– God don't let her be dead, he mumbled softly. He touched both sides of her rib cage, and felt the smallest bit of warmth on her left side.

It wasn't certain that she had died, maybe she was just cold. He pressed his cold fingertips to her slippery, moist fleece and tried to discern a heartbeat. But he didn't feel anything. His fingers were so numb, though, that it meant very little.

Brúska had made her way to him. She looked up at him. She'd stopped stamping, but she flared her nostrils as if winded.

The boy read trust in the grey globes of her ewe eyes. He felt responsible. It wasn't manly to snivel since it was just as likely that the lamb was still alive and numb with cold. The weather wasn't gentle with her, but those little spheres were persistent—she was.

He removed his coat and wrapped it around the lamb. And then he let Brúska sniff the neck of the coat. She nuzzled it, and his sweater too, and bleated sharply, as if she were in pain. It took him aback. He tore off, his arms wrapped around the parcel, and ran as fast as he could home.

But Brúska wasn't being obedient. She often turned back so that he had to run after her, she wandered in all directions. He was constantly stopping and aping the lamb's bleats or stopping to let her sniff the bundle, but it was as if she couldn't hold it in her memory.

The boy was surprised by this stupidity on Brúska's part; he'd always thought she was the most intelligent of all the yearlings, that she would become the bellwether. But she didn't seem to know anything for sure anymore. He was dead tired by the time he got back to the meadow, and paused for a moment's rest against the stone wall, where he examined the lamb more closely.

Now, both of her eyes were open, but they were so strange—they lacked the black, bright circles of pupils. Instead, they were a foggy, blue-gray color, rigid and still, like the frozen sky on a calm morning in Þorri, just before a prevailing wind passes through.

These eyes gave the boy a sense of dread; they weren't the deep, living eyes of a yearling. They were shallow and hard like frost on glass, and they didn't reflect his face.

They merely stared—empty, cross-eyed—and sent a shiver of dread through him, dear lord, the lamb's body had started to stiffen!

Her little legs were rigid like icicles and her neck cracked when he tried to coddle her with his sweater. She had died. The queen of the lambs herself had died. He administered the last rites, and sobbed as her long, soft, eyelashes trembled in the wind like little white wings.

The boy choked down his tears and bleated like a lamb that's lost its mother. It worked well this time; Brúska came galloping, and nearly bowled him over. Then she situated herself a little ways away, wild with bewilderment.

The boy bleated again and extended the lamb's stiff little body toward her. The ewe nuzzled her wet snout against the short-curled slurry of lamb, and cuddled it as before. He coaxed her into the fenced pasture by showing her the lamb and bleating over and over. He no longer found the sound she made ugly. Instead, he despaired when he thought of how she would feel when she realized her lamb was dead. How could he help her understand that not he, but the cold, had killed the lamb—the horrible, biting cold? How would he beg her forgiveness for the death of the queen of the lambs, for all of it? How could anyone endure it?

He sobbed aloud as he lurched the short distance home, overcome by exhaustion. He walked with toes turned inward, and his feet could hardly bear him. He was completely numb from the cold, crying.

– Mamma! He croaked. – Mamma!

The ewe answered him, out in the distance, through the storm.

The morning after, he woke to a fly crawling on his nose. He sat up, began to dress. The frost on the windowpanes had thawed, and water droplets trickled down the glass. They ran in crooked trails, one after another. The water wasn't frozen! His dad had said something about a let-up yesterday evening, but the boy had been so tired that he'd taken in to next-to-none of it. Yes, his dad had definitely said there'd be a break in the weather.

But surely it couldn't be so?

The boy rushed down the dim hallway. When he made it outside, the air was so fragrant that his breaths became heavy. He strode across the yard, and could hardly believe his eyes. He sneezed a few times, inhaled deeply; the intoxicating air filled his nose with a strong, humid perfume.

Newly upsprung cowslips gleamed in his eyes; they spread across the yard, and the farm's grassy flats, as if a generous spring goddess had floated there, sprinkling the polished coins of heaven around the vegetable garden and the ram shed. They were everywhere. The boy gaped at the marvel, made speechless by happiness. He reached out his palm and felt the gentle sprinkle of southern rain flutter into it.

The earth had thawed to the root, and he could almost see flora springing out of the dull ground. Small ponds gathered in stone slabs by the farmhouse door, and a barrel of water in one corner was now filled to the brim, melting ice cubes bobbing on its surface.

It had poured last night. Down in the tussock field, a whimbrel had risen. It strutted grandly up to the highest mound. Then it took wing, letting its long feet dangle. It began to whistle slowly, taking its time:

– Piii – viiiiii. Piii – viiii: long, long. And then it began to gush forth a continuously rising Pi – vii until its long, bowed beak began to open and close so fast that it seemed to the boy it had three bills. The whimbrel was whistling its sputtering song, and it didn't even matter that it was about to spill over.

It was wonderful to hear. Now, winter was over and spring had arrived during the night.

He whooped happily and raced back to the house.

– Gran! He called. Gran! Spring is here! It's really here! It came last night! Your prediction was way off the mark!

The old woman turned in her bed, dug into her stitch muttering and mumbling as she was wont to do. The news seemed to have no effect on her—she didn't even look up.

The boy could discern one sentence in the jumble of words:

– Mark my words, though worms eat my flesh: This will not last long.

It drained the boy's gladness. All at once, he remembered everything that had happened the day before and it darkened his thoughts. He walked the path with a heavy heart and stopped, downtrodden, at the tethering stone next to the barn. Then he looked to the sky, frowning and leery.

Big, billowing rainclouds sailed on a favourable wind across the light blue sea of sky, cutting across the gilded sails of fog. The sun's shining face hid playfully behind silver-grey ripple clouds and a double rainbow forged a bridge from the farm all the way to the sky. A gentle drizzle fell from the sky, and landed on the new growth. Its small, glittering globes trembled on the needle-points of straw before dropping to the greening ground.

The boy saw it all. He looked up at the sky, then turned his gaze back to the ground.

If that wasn't spring, then there was nothing on this Earth you could depend on.

At the very same moment, he heard footsteps, a whistle, and a there we go! from the barn. Then Brúska appeared, a white lamb following close behind her, bleating at her.

The boy rubbed his eyes and gaped. But it was no mistaking it. His dad ambled out of the barn after them as if nothing extraordinary had happened. The dog brought up the rear, looking a little wily.

The boy lost his breath.

– Dad! Dad! Did you revive her? Is she really alive?

His dad smiled.

– Oh, no. She isn't. But old Golsa gave birth to two this morning and we'll see how well Brúska takes to the second one. It's a new queen of the lambs. Now go down to the pasture and look after them.

His dad turned around and disappeared back into the barn before the boy could ask more questions. He realized then that a white lambskin had been slung over the back of the new lamb and fasted under its belly. He understood. They needed to fool Brúska.

He grabbed his crook and set off after her.

The dog laid at the foot of the tethering stone and observed them. The boy thought he looked half-insulted. It occurred to him that he could turn around and pet the pup, but he didn't.

He couldn't do everything at once, so he ran after Brúska, taking care not to trample the cowslips along the way. When he got down to them, he sat on a soft, mossy mound and looked at Brúska and her new queen of the lambs. Brúska was sceptical of the lamb. She kicked it so it fell over when it tried to give suck. Later, she head-butted the little one so violently that the boy thought she might kill it. He tossed his staff from hand to hand and almost cursed aloud. And then he shooed Brúska away with strikes and kicks. But she hopefully plodded right back, her snout lightly sniffing the earth, and she bleated lowly, with a closed mouth. She looked ashamed when she sniffed the lamb. The boy raised his staff, ready to strike.

Brúska looked the lamb over warily, still mistrusting, still questioning. Then she suddenly stroked the little dimwit with her snout and the expression of her eyes lightened. Her long face lit up with wonder, ebullience, and happiness, and she bleated a rumbling noise, like an old ram, and permitted the lamb to suckle.

A little while later, he tried to pet the lamb, but Brúska snorted, backed away, and headbutted him with all of her might. Then she stamped and snorted. She sniffed the lamb and looked at him with deep scorn. The boy thought she looked very stupid. Oh, poor girl. There was no hope she'd ever be clever. She would never become the bellwether—he could see it now.

He felt that there was nothing more for him to do here, and he turned back, despondent and a little mopey. It would have been such fun to see the lamb and to stroke it, to hold onto it. It's just how Brúska was.

He swung his staff and watched a plover pair run across the moor, tittering brightly. He ripped up moss and threw it at them. They flew away and landed a little distance away. The boy heard the call of a bird above his head. This bird said:

– Vipp-ipp, vipp-ipp, vipp-ipp.

It was a snipe, a heraldic bird. It flew higher and higher and rose sharply as if it intended to dive, but arrested its ascent, tilted into a glide, and swooped just over his head.

Its tailfeathers sang, its song long and drawn out like a lonely horse whinnying. Then it wheeled a wide circle away from him: Vipp-ipp, vipp-ipp, vipp-ipp!

The boy watched where it soared in the blue spring sky.

The sun peeked out from behind the silver-grey ripple clouds and smiled so beautifully that the dew on the grass glowed, and all the cowslips shined like little coins cast from nuggets of the sun that had fallen from the sky.

Yes, now spring had really come—no matter what anybody said—though grandma's clothes were rotting, though her feet grew cold, though maggots ate her flesh; even though Brúska had grown stupid and selfish and the dog was miffed and the cat wouldn't venture out, and the queen of the lambs had died. It was spring. The snipe had arrived and had prophesied, and there was a new lamb queen.

Spring had arrived with the sun and the grass and the flowers and the plover and the whimbrel and the snipe.

The boy felt its rays run through him. He hopped on both feet and clapped his hands. Then he somersaulted in the dewy moss. He didn't have time to be a grownup now. There was so much he needed to do first. He needed to chase the cat up the clothesline, he needed to pet the dog and get him to play with the woven rope all around the yard, and, preferably, around the vegetable garden as well. He sprinted home, using his stick as a horse so that he'd go faster, he was so glad, the snipe had forecasted so well.

Sunward snipe of delight.

Translator's note: In the Icelandic, this story is titled "Skerpla", the second summer month on the old Icelandic calendar that begins on a Saturday between the 19th and 25th of May and lasts until a Sunday between the 17th and 23rd of June. I have chosen "Lambing season" over "Skerpla" here in part for clarity, and in part because this month coincides to a large extent with the birthing of lambs in Iceland.

This story also references an Icelandic folk rhyme about the arrival of spring and the calls of various birds that portend both ill and fortune. The significant parts the rhyme alluded to in this story, as captured by Jón Árnason, may be roughly translated as:

*" The heath plover sings summer in,
the snipe composes destiny,
winter ne'er runs its course
until the whimbrel sputter-sings*

Whence one first hears the snipe's whinny foretells what events await. Depending upon where or from which direction the snipe is first heard in spring, the rule goes:

*From the east is heard the snipe of wealth,
from the south, the snipe of happiness,
from the west, the snipe of misery,
from the north, the snipe of prosperity,
from above is heard the snipe of delight,
from below, the snipe of death. "*

LILIES

The sick girl lay on the old divan, which sagged in the middle, and creaked under her every movement. She was asthmatic and had come down with a cold. Her lungs were inflamed, the doctor said; the cough was terrible.

A friend had come to call on her, as a result. She situated herself on a box at the foot of the divan, displacing a jam jar full of withered blooms, though it was now impossible to glean what sort of flowers they had once been. She smoked incessantly, clenching her toes—which she'd lacquered red—in her strappy pumps. The cold of the floor cut through her thin soles.

Burning tobacco slowly saturated the humid and musty room; even the mildew was overpowered by her acrid smoke and the choking reek of Chanel No. 5. The discolored wallpaper, which had once been pastel blue, had peeled off the curved slope of the ceiling and now hung in tatters above the sick girl. It was infested with mould and a thick layer of grime that glinted like snow crystals.

Dull sunbeams cut diagonals through the miniscule cross window, catching dust that twisted in the air. The window itself was dirty and close to the ceiling, as in other braggi, barracks huts the Americans had left behind. Profuse, minute cracks spidered through its panes. Little boys entertained themselves by trying to smash it with pebbles, taking aim with their slingshots. But the glass was double-paned and strong and could bear these small packages, apart from a few chinks. When it was bright out, these sparse ornaments resembled miniature suns and cast coronas. When it was overcast, they became miniature moons encircled by haloes. They luminesced in muted daylight. And in the evening, light cast from the neighbour's gave the panes an even more dramatic aspect; they took on all sorts of colours, and the cracks glowed like tiny stars. The girl was content to watch this spectre until they turned off their lights.

Her friend looked frustrated. They'd been quarreling. She wrung her salmon summer gloves like a dish cloth. A gaunt girl of about thirty, with dyed red hair and purple lipstick. Her boney fingers were heavy with rings, but none of them were that most-sought-after of all rings, the wedding ring. Instead, she wore a cheap collection of glass and stones, the kind that women enjoy buying and showing off. She wore just as many bracelets, which jingled when she wafted away clouds of smoke or secured a cigarette in her decorative holder, the type that American movie stars use.

– But you have to see the specialist, she said. I think you must have a screw loose or something, not taking care of a thing like that. God, I don't know where I'd be if I hadn't had him – I'd be dead!

– But people need someone to love, the sick girl stammered. Not just sometimes, but all day, all night, something to hold close to, something beautiful to hold onto, always. I want to have flowers – they're beautiful and good – and children – they're beautiful and good, too. I want things to be like that – I want to have beautiful things around me.

– Always, now come off it! She cuts her off. What lasts forever? Nothing. If things were forever, I'd still have Jim. I thought we loved each other. God, really! One night, two, bless you! And then he was gone, just like any other soldier, just like yours. You thought you'd always have your little Sissí, even though her pabbi did a runner! Hardly a year old. Then she got that encephalitis and died. One thing after another. And flowers! Who keeps flowers in the clean-picked bones of an old barracks. They belong in nice living rooms, well-kept rooms, the kind that proper people have!

She studied the flowers with scorn and knocked the jar over with her toe. The shriveled blossoms just rustled; their water had long dried up. The vessel rocked roundly on the floor.

– Flowers wither and end up in the trash, and kids get sick and die. You lose one thing after another. But I think Sissí's death was a boon for you.

The sick girl gasped, horrified.

– God, how can you be so awful, she said.

The friend shrugged her shoulders and lit another cigarette.

– Awful? No. I'm just telling it like it is. When pabbi pisses off to America, their babies are better off with God. What are you supposed to do with them? There's no food. Ég er að segja satt. I'm telling the truth. Gosh!

– But I still think that you should have someone to love. I think I'll die without it. It's no life-- achoo! Mine hasn't been a life since my Sissí died, well, not until…

– Start again! So many people have a child and lose it, rich people, too, and then they just stop making altogether.

– Yes, but she was so beautiful and good…

– Now, come on. She was just like other kids. People go through this. Many people. But poor girls, unmarried, shouldn't do things like this – have a child, I mean – and least of all in a braggi. I mean that.

The friend slapped her thigh with her gloves and exhaled sharply. She pretended not to hear the sick girl's whimpering.

–I think it's enough for you to have Nonni, at least you can be content with an Icelander. I really don't understand it – god he's so— I'll never get how can you stand to be with a hairy sailor like that, working down at the docks! God, he's such a pleb. But what's to be done. A guy like him won't waste time packing his bags when you break the news!

The sick girl rose and dried her tears. She was incensed.

– I've already told Nonni, she said. And he wasn't bad about it. He was good. He doesn't want me to go to the specialist. He says we'll find a way.

The other girl touted.

– A way! Easy to say! Find a way! In this useless tin can, and you – without your health, without anything!

You remember what happened to Sissí. Think you're both crazy. Biluð. I say that.

They were both silent for a moment.

Then the sick girl began to whimper, and that whimper grew into a cry, and the cry grew into a wail.

Her friend felt ashamed. She crouched down and set the dried flowers upright, taking care to arrange them as if they were new and alive. Then she sat next to the sick girl and shyly stroked her sweaty, close-cropped hair.

– Gosh, I really feel for you, she whispered. You know I only want the best for you. You have to see that it just isn't possible, nothing is... these are difficult times. I'll come with you to the specialist if you're too shy. Should I do that? Huh? Now, dry your eyes.

Her comforting words burrowed into the sick girl and little by little, her crying slowed.

Finally, she sat up and dried her tears with her fists like a child. She snapped her feet under her; they were cold. Her nose was red, and her face, puffy.

– Give me a smoke, she said, reaching out her hand.

– Of course, love. You should never lose your nerve if you can set something right. The specialist is so easy to talk to, so polite. I don't know how many times he's saved me. You see. It just comes with the territory.

The sick girl followed the trail of smoke with her eyes until it broke apart in the sunbeams. She sniffled. She ceded.

– Maybe I'll just go then, she said finally. But it's all so awful.

Her friend sighed and turned away her eyes, staring absentmindedly at the flowers in the jar.

– I'll come with you, she said, raising her voice like an old man. You put aside money. It's expensive. Nonni will…

The sick girl blew a jet of smoke into the air.

– Yes, I don't have the cash, she said. And what do I say to Nonni? God, what a mess!

– Nonni will get the money, the friend said. He has to.

– Yes, but what do I tell him? How do I explain – it? Nonni has been so good to me.

The doctor wasn't her friend's specialist—she'd arrived in the examination room of her own.

– So, you're back?

– Yes.

– What's going on now?

– So much.

– What is it? Irregularity, vitamin deficiency, love, poverty, nervousness, a cold house…

– Well, yes, but…

The girl fell silent and looked, ashamed, at her hands in her lap.

The specialist looked at the blank form as if he were searching for some clue, and picked at the edge of the table impatiently.

– Well, what is it then? He asked curtly. Tell me what's wrong.

– There's so much.

– A lot, yes, right, yes, but what's troubling you the most?

– I'm so worried about being there in winter. It's so cold and ugly and…

– You just need to get married, my dear. Get an apartment and a man and get married. Then everything will improve and you'll forget what's passed. Everyone has troubles, but every cloud has a silver lining. You need to have strong character, that's it. Absólútt!

The doctor smiled, satisfied he'd solved the problem. He'd settled the matter.

– I'm expecting.

The smile that had congealed on the doctor's face melted into a look of horror. He stared at her with an open mouth, his expression fixed.

The girl was frightened to see his face distort like that. What had she said?

– But this boy, he's good… she jabbered. It's not another 'merican soldier; this one is good, he's not going to leave me, he's just normal, nothing special. He's a dock worker, an Icelander, down by the harbour, he said we'd figure it out, that we would find a way, he said… achoo!

The girl's sneeze stopped her speech. The doctor's face relaxed. He'd now regained his ability to close his mouth, and did so slowly. Then he swallowed.

– It's all true, the girl insisted. He's not a cheat, no, certainly not. He is good.

– Can you – can he not get an apartment and marry you? Then, then everything would be in order…

– He's poor. He only has work sometimes. He doesn't have money for an apartment. And I've started to show. Women spot it right away, and then they don't want to rent to us…

The doctor had, by then, managed to right himself. He arranged forms one on top of the other, lining up their

63

corners just so; and they looked like a single sheet, not a stack.

– Ahem, well. That's... hm… very unfortunate, very awkward. But that's that.

Silence.

– You should have – people should take better care of themselves. Those old barracks aren't any place for a child. And, hm, well, homeless, poor, unmarried…

–Yes, he was in the street. And I… I really care for him, I promised him I'd…

The girl peeked up at the doctor, shyly apologizing with her eyes.

– He's so good.

– Good, right, yes, right, right. Good, yes, yes. But that's not enough. One must have strong character. Absolutely. And poor people, living in braggi… especially them.

The girl's face darkened. Her freckles turned almost black.

– I know you have to take care of yourself…to have care – achoo! – charact…

– Character.

– Yes, but he was so cold on the floor. And the divan is so narrow. And you're so close together. And your hands, they just move themselves.

– Hm, hm.

– I know it's not okay. But he was so good. There are so few good ones. And I couldn't … be bad. The girl stopped speaking. She choked down a sneeze, and her eyes flashed insistence.

The doctor cleared his throat.

– There's nothing more to say than, well, you have to make the best of this, you'll have to marry…and immediately, without hesitation, and you have to get on the national insurance. You might be able to slip in before, hm, before the child is born. How, hm, how far along are you?

– Three months, almost four.

– No, then it's just under. But only by a hair's breadth. You should still be able to get the insurance. You need to get checked out at Stöðin. It doesn't cost anything.

The doctor grabbed one of the forms, and rapidly filled in the blanks. This paper was different than the others. His papers shuffled and the precise organization of the desk was brought to an end in a flash.

– You need to get shots. Vitamins, I mean. And you need to build routines, and try to smoke less.

– I'm trying. But when you're hungry . . .

– Yes, and you need to eat every meal. Absólútt!

The specialist stood up, reinvigorated and authoritative. He handed her the form with an elegant flick of the wrist.

– Well, then. That should take care of it. We hope for the best. But we have to make the best of everything, and have strong character. It's our duty to society. Absólútt. You must speak to the people at the City and see if they can do anything about your heating problem. Maybe they can paint, too. Try to get them to take care of things. And save when and where you can. Don't buy anything unnecessary, nothing fancy for the child – they don't need it. The most important thing is that it's healthy.

– Yes, I'll… we'll do that. Achoo!

The doctor opened the door to his office. He patted the girl on her shoulder as she tried to slip past him.

–You say he's good. There are two of you, and you must help one another. It's very important, of course, to have strong character, but it's perhaps more important to just be good.

The girl had waited at the administrative department of the City, and she'd stood in front of two men named Ólafur and Sveinn. They'd both smiled to her, they'd both been soft and conscientious, and Ólafur had said: Yes, yes, soon, very soon. And Sveinn energetically opined: Yes, yes, of course, of course. And he scribbled something on a slip of some sort and handed it to her.

She'd also stood before a glass edifice and the woman behind it who guarded the money. There, she'd exchanged the slip she'd gotten from Sveinn for a large banknote. It was stiff and peaty yellow, but now it had been broken into many smaller crumpled bills in blue and red and green. And those bills had been scattered here and there.

First, the shop with the bird—a large bird, and intelligent, with a big red beak and wrinkled, red feet. It's as if he knows something, even lords over an important secret, but he's closed-mouthed and determined to keep it to himself. A bird of that sort.

A few had gone to the florist next door to Gosi. There was just something about that shop. Flowers grow more beautiful in bleak surroundings. Sometimes, you can find flowers there on the cheap. And you never feel shy inside, even if you're a little shabby. It's a good store.

Another few went to the clothing store. There was such a lovely robe in the window. It was nothing more than calico, but awfully nice, in bright and cheerful colors. She couldn't resist.

A few had gone to Clausen's. Even when you're full to the gills, your mouth still waters when you look in that window. As she stood in line, the girl felt terribly hungry. And when it was her turn to order, she bought everything she had wanted and more.

The money was gone as quickly as it came. And now there were only a few fivers and one ten. The girl clutched a few coins in her sweaty palm. She had needed them for the bus, but decided instead to save the money and walk. The people around town were so elegant and well-dressed, and the weather was so clear.

When she turned off Túngata, a cool sea wind sprinted toward her all the way from Hofsvallagata. The sun lit up the sea, the sun whitened the clouds, the sun turned the sky azure. The sun was so bright in the fathomless sky that the girl had to look away from it—toward the villas that looked like distant fairytale palaces by the fjord. She ran her eyes over a dark strip that sliced across the lightning-white backdrop to the west. The strip had the look of smoldering ruins, as if the villas that had once stood there had burned to cinders—squat black pillars jutted out of the rubble like scorched limbs pointing toward the heavens.

But the girl knew them well and smiled to herself and hurried on her way.

They weren't ruins. Not at all. It was just the barracks, the neighborhood she now called home. No villas had been burned. People lived there; real, live, working people. She lived there—the two of them lived there. He would come home tonight, her man. And soon they'd be three!

Her heart warmed at the thought, and she cradled her parcels closer. When she met a fine lady, she straightened up a little to lead with her belly ; she forgot she didn't have a ring and that everyone could see it.

The sea wind brushed her short boyish hair, her freckled face. But she felt fine and rich. Some of her packages even contained things those women didn't have, like tiny baby underclothes and a pink knitted onesie and a sweater—and a little nightgown, white with pink embroidery on the chest. Three clever little birds singing on a branch. One was the littlest.

And, and how lovely they are! How wonderful it would be to show Nonni all of this! The robe, the little clothes from the bird store—and the flowers!

She'd bought Lilies for him—for them both. They should go in the milk bottle on the box by the divan so they can look at them to brighten their spirits before they go to sleep. Then they won't have to look at the cracks in the window.

The Lilies were pure white, and subtly transparent in their delicacy. She couldn't wait to peek into their paper wrapping.

Resplendent flowers! Regal Lilies, they're called. It was a marvel that they'd sprouted from the dark soil!

SPRING OUTSIDE

Sunlight sparkled through the grimy windowpanes, baking the dust-saturated and discoloured furniture. The mugginess of the living room had become unbearable. Miss Valborg had just begun to struggle with the single window that still opened when she remembered the bird. Namely, that it wasn't in its right place—it wasn't in its cage—it was loose, flitting a restless flight back and forth across the living room. Just then, it landed on the heavy gilded frame of the family portrait. It was quite the opposite of still in its agitation of motion, jerking its neck and shaking its tail. But it didn't once occur to it to sing. Miss Valborg out of habit, lifted her hand to her heart: My goodness! If it... She was petrified of the damage it might do to the frame.

Miss Valborg climbed off her chair with a heavy sigh. It was difficult, this bird. It was only mannerly when it was in its cage.

But Miss Lína had said that it needed to move; it needed to fly around every now and then, otherwise it wouldn't sing for her.

The hope that her bird would sing kept Miss Valborg afloat through all this bother. Miss Lína was perceptive about such matters. Potted plants, goldfish, canaries, budgies—these were her specialties.

But sweet Jesus, getting him back in the cage! That wasn't child's play. The first time, she had to get the entire family to help—wife, daughter, maid, father, and their boys. The husband had caught the bird, in the end.

God, she'd been so frightened for that little beggar in the man's big fist. But providentially, the bird had come out unscathed; it was just a little shaken, and took to cowering atremble in the farthest corner of the cage. You could watch its heart hammering in its little chest. Miss Valborg was so afraid after this event that she didn't dare make another move before fetching Miss Lína.

– It's all okay, Miss Lína said. It's just a little afraid of you now, since there are so many. It will right itself in no time.

And it did right itself in no time. In the evening, the bird had seemingly calmed down. It sat unmoving in the corner, its beak tucked under its wing, even before Miss Valborg came along with the dark green velvet cloth and laid it over the cage. The little beggar was spent.

It had gotten such a fright.

Miss Lína had been wrong in one regard. She said that the bird would acclimate to its enclosure and, as time passed, go in of its own volition. All her birds had done so. But this one did not. It never seemed to get used to the birdcage. It went berserk when she caught it and placed it inside, and it wouldn't settle down for quite a while, even

72

after she'd locked it in the cage with figs and birdseed and water in a dainty porcelain dish.

She often heard it flapping fitfully under the green velvet cloth after she herself had gone to bed and switched off the light. It was grating to her ears; its wings made a terrible rustle when they brushed the bars, and its swing ticked irregularly as it swung. It was like a haunting. She imagined a restless specter roving in the darkness.

Miss Valborg took two extra sleeping tablets and assured herself, over and over, that it was just a bird.

Indeed, Miss Lína had been wrong. The bird never went into the cage willingly and never seemed to get used to it. The exact opposite of what she'd said.

It was the most wonderful cage you could imagine. It was American, originally worth six-hundred Icelandic kronur at the U.S. army base. She'd gotten it for four hundred— the seller couldn't use it, it was too small for their budgies, which had to live in doubles or groups; otherwise, they'd die of boredom. At least that's what Miss Lína had said. This cage was for one bird, and one bird alone, though it was brilliantly made and beautiful.

The bars were made of brown and green plastic to imitate tree branches, and they even had leaves. The illusion was so well done that the bars seemed, at first glance, to be living.

A tiny plastic swing, which looked like red and purple ivy, dangled inside the cage. The bird could enjoy a good swing on it and, preferably, sing while it did so.

There was a little nest of flame-red raffia with snow-white woodwool; a miniature plastic egg, speckled and wonderfully cute, rested inside it. No bird could weave such a divine nest.

Then there was the blue-green porcelain bowl of clear water, a spoonful of white sand in the bottom. This was the bird's miniature bathtub—because they have to bathe themselves. She'd also loaned it her white sugar pot for its drinking water.

She couldn't fathom that it would be so dirty and crass that it'd drink the same water it bathed in. But she'd also never seen it bathe, though Miss Lína had said that it would do so once it felt at home.

But Miss Lína could be mistaken, she saw that now. Because the bird never made itself at home in the cage—this wonderful, American cage—it never went inside without a fight, let alone of its own accord, and it never slept in the nest, never landed on the swing. Even though it had been there all through the winter, and now spring.

And it hadn't sung once.

She'd fought long and hard. After the living room had been in complete disarray four times to capture the bird, Miss Valborg knew that she couldn't go on like this. She had to find a more convenient method than rallying the troops each time she needed to get this unruly bird back into its cage. She sought out Miss Lína for advice.

– You need to get yourself a big net, Miss Lína said.

– A net? Miss Valborg exclaimed.

– A net, Miss Lína repeated. A net—not a big trawl like the ships use, but one of those little ones, like fishermen use.

Miss Valborg gaped. A trawl, well then!

Miss Lína advised her to go to Outdoorsman and ask for a net, a large net.

She went the next day. The man behind the counter smiled, and she got her hands on one. The net was by no means small—and it was only now that she'd gotten the hang of it.

The bird was rocking impishly atop a portrait of the leader of the independence movement, Jón Sigurðsson himself. Miss Valborg found it disgraceful.

She slipped her hand behind the dresser and pulled out the net. She could clearly remember the first time she'd used it. All the pictures on the dresser had been swept onto the floor, their glass panes smashed to smithereens. And two porcelain dogs, too, and a statuette of a couple dancing—a gift from a friend.

Owning a bird that day had been expensive. But now she'd gotten used to maneuvering the net. The bird feared the net more than anything—except for the cage. It darted away from the image and pumped its terrified wings as hard as it could. It slammed into the door's glass, stunned for a moment, dropped to the ground with a dull thump. It never seemed to learn that glass was not open air, no matter how many times it slammed the glass in its attempts to reach freedom. This time, the collision was so hard that it landed limp on the floor. Miss Valborg raised her hand to her heart; she thought it'd been knocked out. But then it started to thrash.

Its beautiful spring plumage swept the floor as it struggled to take flight again. It was a gut-wrenching sight to behold. Miss Valborg reached for it, but that only rewoke its strength. In two quick despairing beats of its wings, it made its way behind the neatly embroidered God-Bless-This-Home wall hanging. It cowered there on the dusty nail, twisted into itself, its wings snapped together—as if the nail were this little persecuted prisoner's last sanctuary. Miss Valborg flipped the net over the whole lot, the bird and the banner. She closed her hand around the shaking animal and shoved it into its cage. It faltered to the farthest corner and stared at the hand that closed the door. Its little beak opened and closed in turns, as if it were begging forgiveness.

Miss Valborg stuck the net behind the dresser and wiped the sweat from her brow, cracking the window. Finally, a breath of fresh air. It was difficult, this bird. It wasn't your typical house bird; not a canary, a parrot, or anything of that sort. This one was an Icelandic redwing thrush.

Miss Lína had caught it at some point in the late autumn and given it to her.

– No, nobody needed to tell her twice: Its boredom with solitude and refusal to get used to the cage were forms of rebellion, too.

The next day was Sunday.

The spring weather was as wonderful as it could get. Everyone who could go outside did so. Miss Valborg had been sitting in the sun in the garden for a while when the loud titter of a bird drilled into her ear canal. This twittering was so full of unbridled merriment and playful joy it charged the air with an energy almost magical.

The music continued to shimmer and shine long after this merry singer had flown away. Miss Valborg's chest gave a sudden jolt, as if a maniacal jazz band were playing a funeral dirge. It was outrageous to feel so flightly Maybe she'd just been startled. She gripped her chest with both of her hands.

– This ruddy noise! Jesus that made me jump! She called out.

Then her eyes landed on a little brown and red bird in the redcurrant bushes just in front of her. It looked at her with dark, fearful eyes and flew away as soon as she pointed her gaze at it. It twinned her bird.

Then she remembered the little wretch who was locked in the dim, cramped living room in this beautiful weather. Why not set the cage outside for a little while and let it breathe some fresh air?

She went inside to fetch the cage, and a moment later, set it down in the green grass, the sun shining on its fake branches, and a breeze playing in the synthetic vines.

Even though it was a real American cage and its branches looked alive in the living room, it was surprisingly dull out here in the blades of grass among the redcurrant bushes. There was something utterly unnatural, vain, and artificial about it; it reminded her of fake flowers on a grave or an electric candle next to a burning flame.

And the bird was acting timid, as if it were ashamed. Maybe it was cold. Maybe it would catch pneumonia. Even though spring was all around, and the sun was hot, its warmth saturating the air. A little while outside hopefully wouldn't do any harm. She would ask Miss Lína about it this evening. She sat back down on her lawn chair and took up her sewing.

Then something wonderful happened: The bird sang!

First, a quiet, shy, hesitant titter as if it were determining whether it still had a voice. Then it swelled into a little efflorescent trill, just like the other bird's song. The tones hung in the air for a second and shimmered and shone like a fishing line. The bird quieted and tilted its head as if it couldn't believe its own ears. A moment passed. Then it began to sing its thrush melody from the beginning—prelude, intermezzo, refrain, and all—he laid his little soul and his little body into this one hot, wild, magical song. He swayed his short tail and stretched out his rust-red neck, glided lightly up onto the artificial ivy, and lifted his head once again in song.

Never had such a song been heard in this garden. Nor in the neighboring gardens. What's more, all the other thrush chaps who were building their nests and other tasks quieted, searching their surroundings resentfully.

Where was this gentle-voiced rival?

And the thrush lady with marriage in mind, who was practically engaged to the promising gentlemen there in the garden, listened dumbstruck. She listened and stared and listened and stared.

Could it be that this wondrous, artful song came out of this laughable hovel on the lawn? She turned her cheek toward it and craned her neck to see better. No, there was no mistaking it. This wondrous singer was inside the cage.

Now it let loose a new aria, and the maiden meandered closer. It raised and lowered its voice entire octaves along the springing lines of song. It was a pleasure to hear. When it reached high C, she couldn't endure it any longer. She moved as close to the singer as she dared. The branch that she landed on rocked gently in the breeze, nearly touching the troubadour's prison.

And when the aria ended, the maiden released the tiniest titter, which was admittedly unobtrusive, but so full of rapture and love that the little brown prisoner's heart jumped and its dark eyes flashed like a struck flint.

The merry angels of paradise had never known the jubilation that now filled the mind of these, their earthly brethren.

It was the euphoria of love.

The cage disappeared to the bird, and he was free. Free in the endless expanses of spring. Below him, fragrant soil threaded thick with green grass and incadescent blooms, and his swing became a treebranch with living leaves and tantalizing buds where he rocked himself in time with his song. There was no petty porcelain bowl filled with tepid, stagnant slop. There were clear, cold springs that streamed in a dreamy murmur and still deep waters that looked up at the blue sky in eternal calm.

His home was in the most beautiful birch in the spinney, where his wife watched over their young in their nest. She was the most beautiful thrush madam that eyes had ever beheld, and he was singing for her. The world was tall and wide and the day was bright, and the sun was warm and good. And soon, night would come, the wondrous respite and protector of all of the birds.

This night wasn't the disturbingly dark drape that was cast by capricious hands over the barred walls of the prison, but rather a blue, deep and calm, full of peace and security under the restful eyes of stars, cool breath.

This night wasn't a dusty, choking rag that blinded and ensnared, but the gentle wings of a mother that, with love and stewardship, embraced little, drowsy thrush families in their modest bed.

A world-famous heldentenor had never entranced his audience as completely as this feathered, dark-eyed genius entranced the beautiful thrush maiden from behind the bars of his prison on the grass that sun-warmed day. To say that he sang his way into her heart, as the newspapers put it, would be an understatement; no, he had completely possessed her in form and feather.

Her love and infatuation became more powerful than her trepidation over this hovel. She sacrified the security of the branches and darted over to the cage, where she could kiss him between the bars—not just thank him for the song, but for his existence, for their existence, and this spring.

He began his recital, singing one song after another; first came the classics, with classic themes like the sweetness of love, the contentedness of family life. Then, dance and pop tunes about fleeting happiness, jolly carrion flies and fat earthworms, fragrant seeds and sweet honey. All of this, he intended to conjure and give to her, if she would only accept him. And she wanted so truly to be his. She had plain forgotten the promising thrush gentleman who had secured a location for their nesting in the maple tree by the path.

She was completely won over by the gorgeous song of her new friend. Its artistry carried more weight than its competitor's means and status. The thrush maiden peeped and chirruped with satisfaction and hopped and turned circles around the cage. The prisoner sang again with his whole heart and spread out his beautiful feathers and swished and swayed on the fake vines. Despite the bars, he managed to treat her to figs and a few grains of birdseed.

Oh, how he longed to go out!

But that wasn't possible. This American enclosure was Super Solid and sturdy. A little bird has so few options inside the walls of this type of cage; he can only sing a little about the world outside.

Miss Valborg listened to the song in the cage. She found it wonderful—perhaps because the singer was her bird, and because it had now sung for the very first time. Now, it was more likely to comply, to make itself amenable. Then she'd be free of all the net-fussing and struggle and nerve-wracking nonsense that had come along with her possession. Now it would make itself at home in the cage and she didn't need to listen to its fidgety fluttering in the thick darkness of night, when it should've been sleeping. She could get along with the old dosage of her sleeping pills and her fear of the darkness would disappear, too.

Now it would be an obedient and orderly bird that gave her the hours of pleasure she so longed for. It might even become so docile that it'd lay eggs next to the sweet plastic egg in the golden nest, and these would hatch perfect, adorable young.

Miss Valborg flushed at the thought. She smiled shyly to herself and tried to avoid thinking about this any further. She focused on her needlework. It would be such fun to tell Miss Lína all this evening.

The bird was ill. It cowered motionless in one corner of the cage, so small that the cage seemed far outsized for its tiny form. Up to this point, it had always seemed too small to contain the creature. Miss Valborg sat with her hands folded, looking at the bird in bewilderment. She'd tried everything. All that advice from the husband and the maid, from the housewife and their boys, and their friends in the office. It had all come to naught. It worsened with each passing hour.

There was just one more bit of advice she could try out; Miss Lína's. She had put it off as long as she could; it was all so sickening, so grim.

The misfortune had been set in motion on that memorable Sunday when she'd taken it outside—though she didn't know then what she was getting into. She had set the cage outside each day in good weather, and after that, the bird was completely deflated indoors. Her hope that it would get its act together if it were allowed to go outside had disappointed. In those first days, it had come back to life—it gathered its seeds with gusto and, indeed, hopped up onto the little swing and tittered happily for a while.

But it would only sing outside. There, it was just like another bird, a bird she didn't know. To her, the bird grew and beautified.

But then she came upon its secret. It was carrying on with that nasty naughty boy bird that loitered in the redcurrant bushes. There was something indecent about that bird. She had seen how hers behaved around it. Miss Valborg simply wouldn't tolerate such crass nonsense.

Men!

It drove its head between the bars as far as it would go, and spread its wings and wiggled. It was vulgar.

She had believed that her bird in the cage—which was certainly a ladybird, Miss Lína had said—was, in fact, civilized in this area, like all females of a better sort. But this civility was not the case.

It was apparent that this filthy thrush was enjoying this obscene importunity; she was no better herself.

The nerve!

Miss Valborg couldn't bear the sight. She moved the cage away with righteous indignation, away from the fragrant grass, away from the glistening sunshine and the singing breeze and shoved it into the dimmest corner of the living room. She was so angry that she sought the green velvet drape and cast it rashly over the cage. There you shall stay.

Then she sat down to her sewing and tried to regain her composure. But little came from her work. Through the skin-thin velvet cloth, she heard the despairing, pleading titter and restless rustling. She sensed that the bird was begging her for freedom—for life and for the spring outside, begging to be with the other birds and sing in the majesty out, outside.

Never, ever!

Miss Valborg jerked a thread and snapped it.

Such filthy business! If it couldn't be cordial, then it would stay inside. The tittering in the cage finally stopped. But the rustling went on. Those little wings stroked the bars, those slender, but merciless bars that closed off life and brightness, that locked freedom out. It searched and searched for a passage in its shivering stupor.

Where was the passage, this minute door that sometimes opened to freedom?

Miss Valborg jumped to her feet. How could she be afraid of the dark on such a dog day? No, it would never go out again to play its games, not like last time.

That time, it had been so despondent when she brought it in that she took pity and opened the cage to let it fly around the room for a while.

It cowered in a corner with its eyes closed and hung its wings. It usually jetted out when she opened the cage. Now, it didn't stir. It opened the slits of its eyes when it heard the soft motion of the door and closed them again. But now it didn't move at all. Perhaps it believed it was dreaming. Perhaps it had given up hope of freedom. Miss Valborg poked it with her finger. That stirred it to flutter out. At first, it seemed that it didn't know how to fly anymore. But then it lifted into the air and disappeared. Miss Valborg had absentmindedly left the door to the hall open.

Mercifully, the older boy had been messing around with something in the hallway, oriented himself to the situation, and took immediate action. He grabbed the bird just as it reached the open window and held it proudly up to Miss Valborg's nose.

The bird thrashed, but the boy held fast. It had no effect. This was the thanks she got for showing charity. Miss Valborg slammed the cage door and slung the cloth over. The nerve!

It took ill after that. It didn't even look at the treats she put in its cage, but merely curled together in the corner and hung its head and wings. Its eyes were always closed. It was unkempt and scraggly. It cut Miss Valborg to the quick to watch it rot away like this. What could she do?

She'd tried everything.

One sunny day, she armed herself with a long-shafted feather duster that she used to dust the picture frames and the porcelain, and headed out into the garden. She was going to chase that vulgar chap out of the garden so that her bird would be safe from temptation. Then it could be in the grass, unperturbed by vulgarity and importunity.

She launched a fierce onslaught on the redcurrant bushes where the miscreant hung about, shrieking and setting upon them. A whole flock of little, brown, frightened birds swarmed out of the bushes. They were all the same. It was hardly possible to pick out the right one.

Miss Valborg thought it a shame to have to frighten all of them, but there was nothing else to be done. The innocent sometimes suffer with the guilty.

But her labors amounted to nothing. The birds returned with just as much force, and disappeared into the foliage. She watched one of them retrieve a big, fat earthworm from the soil right at her toes. Another ran the same errand just after the first.

Miss Valborg filled with loathing. She resigned herself. She shouldered the feather duster and turned toward the house. It was a hopeless labor. The birds' home was there, their nests and their young. They would always come back. They would always return, even if she stood there all night, screeching and striking.

How aborrhent! Such a nature!

Yes, what a troublesome battle.

Miss Valborg wanted to cry. She really cherished the bird, despite its foibles and its shortcomings. She'd cherished it so much more since it became ill. She had hoped and begged that it would be civil and decent, and give her pleasure and gladness, like a normal bird. Like Miss Lína's birds.

They'd been raised well.

But that's not it; she had tried to raise that bird well, though it hadn't borne fruit yet. Because it was rebellious, fussy, capricious; it never wanted to sing inside and had flaunted its indecency in public.

Nature did that. The rebellious Icelandic nature. Foreign birds never behaved this way. Maybe it couldn't help it. And she was ready to forgive it for everything in an instant, if it would just become well again. If it lived, there was hope.

What did the priest say on Sunday:

– 'Where there's life, there's hope of contrition.' Those were his exact words.

If it would only live.

But now she had tried everything—everything. Except Miss Lína's advice.

Imagine, Miss Lína saying a thing like that!

– Try to give it earthworms, she'd said.

Earthworms! How disgusting! Imagine a prim and proper bird swallowing such a foul thing!

But wild thrushes did. She'd seen it herself. She'd always been particularly disguisted by earthworms. They were ungodly creatures. But it wasn't worth wracking her brains over. She needed earthworms, that was the final piece of advice she'd gotten. If only the boys had been home. But they were at their summerhouse with their parents. She couldn't wait. She had to do it herself.

She took an old sweeties tin she'd used as a button box, emptied it, and headed to the shed. There, she found work gloves that were a few sizes too big for her hands and put them on. Then she took a large spade, dragged it behind her to the garden, and began to dig.

She felt as if the tin were squirming in her hands as she carried it inside. It was no wonder; it was full of big, repulsive worms, five of them, or ten rather. She couldn't imagine setting them alive into the cage, that clean, fine cage, or watching them squirm, spreading their slime and mud all through it.

So she had taken aim at them with the spade, closed her eyes, and sliced them clean in half. One end had to be their heads. After she'd cut them all in two, this didn't turn out to be true: their heads were either on both ends, or they didn't have heads. Because each of what were now ten worms squirmed and floundered furiously. They slithered away with great speed, each in its own direction. She had tried to trample them to death, but that only enlivened them. In all likelihood, these creatures couldn't be killed.

She screwed up her courage and dropped them into the bag with a broken fork.

To her, the bag squirmed as if it were alive, and she tossed it aside in revulsion. She felt nauseated. She stepped away and threw up.

It was all for nothing.

She had let the bag open in the cage and washed herself meticulously. Then she sat down and waited. The worm-stubs were as lively as ever; she hoped they wouldn't writhe out of the tin.

The bird remained still in its corner. Its eyes were closed and it didn't move an inch. Miss Valborg gave it a minute. Then she lost patience. She opened the cage and poked the bird. It shifted the slightest bit and tried to lift its wings.

It might still get scared. Its eyes were like two black spheres and the fear shone in them. Its little mouth opened and it peeped the tiniest peep. It was like the crisp tone in a crystal glass that's just as quickly snuffed out with your hand.

Then it fell on its side. It tried once more to lift the wing that faced the sky. Then it lay still.

Miss Valborg wheezed a quiet whine and lifted the little corpse. She no longer felt its quick, frightened heartbeat in the palms of her hands. Her bird was dead. She set it aside on the wardrobe after thinking to herself for a moment. There was no danger of losing it now.

Its flights could no longer do any harm. The little body would no longer thrash, the feet were powerless, the wings hung limp. Yes, there was no danger of losing it, though the door was open.

Miss Valborg sank into her chair and lifted her hand to her heart out of habit. But there was a new discomfort in her chest. She had never felt anything like it before. It was something of a completely different nature.

She could visualize the open hole in the garden, a small black hole. It didn't fit in with the green grass around it; it was tragic beside the bright flowers. It was grave and taciturn under trees that shook in the breeze, tittering with cheerful birdsong. This hole was menacing, cruel, and greedy, though it wasn't very large. As in the dirge, the worms that ate the flesh lived there. She had met those worms today.

Their worm does not die – now who said that? Not Miss Lína. Someone else had said it.

Others lived in the trees. Birds that forever returned for their young in their nests. All those little, poor nests, all those dark eyes peering from within the thick of green leaves and up into the blue sky.

She felt these eyes glare at her from every direction. The dead bird glowered. Its eyes were the eyes of all the other birds—the eyes of the young, the eyes of the vulgar bird in the redcurrant bushes—the eyes of life, though they were dead and couldn't see.

These eyes had been meant to look out upon the world and see all of its wonder, to sense love, spring, and life, not to be blinded by a dusty cloth in a vain American cage, shut in by walls of hopeless darkness.

Miss Valborg looked at the bird. It was as if she saw it alive for the first time, though it'd begun to stiffen.

This wasn't her bird. She didn't own it, she had no right to make it sing for her, no right to take anything from it.

It was life to which it belonged; its own life of love, and happiness, and song. It belonged to the spring outside.

And now, it was dead. Miss Valborg wept.

Then she realized, all at once, what it was—that unidentifiable feeling of discontent in her chest, that she hadn't realized was there. It was a hole like the one in the garden, a dark hole full of slimy earthworms, deep and taciturn and vicious and greedy. It was a grave dug for dead birds, that had died in a cage and would sing nevermore.

SUNDAY NIGHT TO
MONDAY MORNING

If anyone had seen how they looked at me just before I left—how those women turned to one another as they strode past me—they would've concluded:

— So that's the guilty one—the harlot herself.

How could they have possibly understood me?

They leaned into their husbands' ears—conservatively groomed, their hair swept tidily back, their faces modestly painted—and whispered conspiratorially to them. Each has loved one, and only one, man.

I looked like a tart, and I was tantalized by every man in the room; I gripped my seat to hold myself back from hurling myself into their arms.

I fixated on one man's hair. Overcome by temptation, I made my move to sit with him.

— How very bold, he said. Get lost.

As I lowered myself into the adjacent seat, he rose out of his. His hair swished and swayed like an ocean of lustrous wire.

I seized it, coiled it around my fingers, pulling hard with both of my hands.

It was so pleasurable that I didn't notice the roar building up around me—I heard only a dull hum flush out of the women in the room, the subtle crash of glass breaking around me.

I felt his neck bow under the power of pain. Soon it would be mine, I would purify my hands in this churning ocean of hair.

He jerked as I tightened my grip, reveling in its persistence—certain I would never lose it, not even for a second—I would sooner surrender my life. I felt another set of fingers wrap around my own, bend them back as if to break them.

I didn't notice the pain as my hand was pried open. Two men—the owner of the hair and another—dislodged my right hand from the ocean, but as they did so, I grabbed hold with my left. And so it went on for a while. It didn't occur to anyone that I had more than one hand.

I was calm, certain I would win the war and make off with this singularly precious object.

I didn't feel how they twisted and tugged at my fingers.

I didn't need to pay them any mind because my hands sought his hair just as they were severed from it.

Then, I felt an awful pain. Somebody was tearing my hand apart; they ripped my thumb from my palm. The shaft of my arm was sheared from its socket.

— Stop it, shewolf, the owner of the hair hissed.

I didn't want to let go, but I crawled my hands, sheepish, out of his hair—a few iridescent copper threads clung to my fingers.

The arm of my dress was ripped at the seam. I was shoved to the floor, which was sopping and strewn with erratic glass.

I felt how it stabbed through my clothes, cracked into my body.

The master of the house carouselled over me, gross, insult crossing his face—a strange moon.

He grabbed my arm and dragged me.

— Scram. I don't want streetwalkers in here. You're not welcome. My wife and I would never let in such, such trash.

The stairway opened its charcoal mouth to swallow me alive. I sensed that the bottom was far, far below. A violent dread gripped me, and I reached for the wrist of my persecutor. I wanted to beg for clemency, to repent, but the sobs in my throat occluded my supplications. I was crashing toward a dire dark—all my life plunging, plunging, and at the very bottom is tar, a tarpit where rodents welter in ooze, thrashing and scratching with teensy, tiny feet, wrestling against death. The tar drinks in the soft strands of their fur and fills the globes of their big, black eyes—I was teetering, about to fall, when someone wrapped an arm around my waist and caught me.

— Don't throw her out—if you throw her out, you'll have to throw me out, too. She's one of my models. You've got her shaking like a frightened animal.

They tugged me back and forth.

— Just leave her alone, those glasses aren't worth a dime.

He helped me into a chair.

I didn't dare look up — tears streamed down my cheeks and out of my nose in a constant flow. As they puddled in my lap, the velvet of my garments drank them in. I thought of an irrigation ditch I'd once dug.

I didn't want them to see me cry. I fixed my gaze on the carpet, where the broken glass had been just a moment before.

Most of the shards had been swept up, but the wine spills were still damp.

I began to cry because everything was so sad and so tragic—the glasses would never be whole again, the wine would never be drunk, the uprooted strands stuck to my fingers would never again be strung to their harp.

Inside of me, I was told that I deserved a slow and painful drowning in the tarpits, among the poor little mice who'd never done anything wrong.

Me, a murderer, a thief, a harlot.

A panel of judges surrounded me, loomed over me. They were serious, severe, sage-like. I stretched defenseless before them, pierced through by the intensity of their gaze. On my soul they tallied my crimes, as if it were an open ledger.

I curled into a ball of anguish, my frame shaking with the force of my sobs. I knew begging for mercy was pointless, but it crossed my mind as a last resort; criminals are sometimes granted reprieve. I held my breath, waited.

One of the judges transfigured into an angel in a pair of glasses. She supported me all the way to the bathroom and stroked my hair out of my eyes.

— I started to cry because you were crying, she said as she dried my tears with the back of her sleeve, and I

96

watched as her eyes welled up behind the lenses of her glasses.

I leaned on her and listened to her heartbeat. Only then did I feel the great pain of my sins. The woman whose heart was beating next to my ear was such a good girl. I confessed to her and she granted absolution, not thinking of the mess I'd made of her dress, and I wasn't alone any longer; alongside me, I had one of the good angels.

God had been thoughtful like that.

But then she vanished, and I searched for her, sobbing all the while, but instead found another judge who'd transformed into a different being. A sailor.

— Are you crying, Ásta? But you're the strongest of us all.

He stroked my cheek with his big hand.

— Who has hurt you so? I'll punch him in the gizzard— the kisser, I mean.

— Nobody hurt me, I whimper.

— We'll stand by you, my dear Ásta, the big man swore, moved to tears.

— Don't go out in the dark, not by yourself. I'll come with you. It's not safe alone.

He ran to fetch his coat.

For a while I waited, listening for footsteps on the stairs. It was a tall and dangerous staircase and one had to tread carefully. I waited and waited but nobody came, and I set off to find the people who had wandered off before me. The streets were empty and eerily quiet. The buildings had closed their eyes and fallen fast asleep. Streetlamps stood guard in the darkness like lonely sentinels, without so much

as blinking. A portentous silence fell. My footsteps echoed darkly off the cement cliffs around me.

I stopped at the window of a keepsake shop on the corner of Austurstræti and Aðalstræti. Only then did it occur to me that the streets weren't covered in snow, and that there were no footprints stomped into them. I couldn't trace a single track, and nobody could find me. I'd left nothing behind to lead them to me. I realized that the world I'd been searching for was gone, all joy was gone, and all company was gone.

I'd been thrown to the outermost edge of the darkness because of my sins, and sooner than I'd expected. God would not forgive me. I understood how Jesus felt on the cross when he'd called out to God and asked why he had left him alone. I was alone, too, and lost, hopeless, even Jesus had forgotten how he'd felt on the cross, even he'd forgotten me. Things were going well for him up in heaven.

I had nowhere to rest my head, nowhere to listen to the paced heartbeat of another being and close my eyes and fall to sleep.

I was damned to eternal wakefulness under these glowing, glaring streetlights.

I began to cry again, loudly and violently, like a terrified child who has lost her mother and sees the darkness beginning to gather.

The sound bounced from one stone colossus to another, echoed from distance to distance.

I laid down in the street and sprawled out and surrendered all defenses and closed my eyes so I would not see the thing I feared the most.

I heard footsteps from around the corner. I held my breath to hear better.

God must have forgiven me and sent another comforter. It wasn't long before he ambled in my direction.

It was a middle-aged man, a kind-looking man. He came to a halt and jumped back when he saw me lying there. Then he bent down, lifted my chin.

— Did you hurt yourself, little darling? He asked.

— No, no.

— Why are you crying so?

— I'm not sure.

— You're a pretty little thing, he said. Let's go to my place, where you can wash those tears off your face. He lifted me to my feet and took hold of my arm. Men are good.

Suddenly, I was in a luxurious parlor, with a fresh face and tidied hair. A crystal flute, filled to the brim with champagne, glistened next to a tray of sandwiches.

My comforter had removed his coat and I noticed for the first time how obese he was. He shot me a paternal smile as he leaned back in his chair, which released a homey creak under his weight. He lit a mammoth cigar and squinted at me.

— There's something about you, he said. You're a rare one, my dove.

He drummed on the table with his fingertips. He looked like he was about to dictate business correspondence.

— Where did you get those eyes? I've never seen such beautiful eyes. He exhaled a monstrous jet of smoke, and looked me up and down.

— What color are they? Can they see the future?

I couldn't answer. Instead, I cowered behind the flute of champagne. All was silent for a moment.

He cleared his throat.

— What do you do, little darling? He asked.

— I'm a model, I replied, my voice livelier.

— Well, well, a model? What is that now? He asked, a little surprised.

— I sit for people who draw. I sit naked on a stool, or on the floor, I said, straightening.

— Yes, I see, he said. Sometimes I paint and sketch.

He pointed to the wall.

— These are my works, he gloated. They're my imaginings.

I looked up at a monumental picture in a gilded frame. It was of a young girl in a skimpy bikini, with large breasts and a waist no wider than her scrawny neck. She was holding a fishing pole. In the background, a purple mountain, a placid lake, and a racing boat. She was surrounded by roses. It was very amateurish.

There were a few smaller pictures with the same strokes and similar motifs. I startled when, out of the blue, he said:

— Will you take off your clothes, so that I can see your figure? Maybe you'll be my model.

— Okay, sure. I felt relieved that I could repay his kindness. He'd done so much for me. I heard him suck in his breath.

— Hurry up a bit, my darling, he said.

I gulped down the rest of my champagne and went into the bathroom to undress.

My dress was all torn, I noticed, my blouse was almost the whole way off, the arms and neck ripped at the seams. It was my best dress.

I removed my garments slowly because my hand was tender where the judges had splayed it. Finally, I stood naked in the tiled bathroom and ran my hands down my body. I was not free from the shame of comparison: my body in relation to the girl in the painting. I was too thick, my breasts were too small and I wasn't fashionable and the hair on my pubic bone didn't form a perfect triangle—

He walked into the bathroom, naked. The good man had turned magenta, his face had swelled. He rolled his eyes and, hands trembling, reached for me. His potbelly hung down to his knees, his breasts dangled like two sacks from his hairy chest and jiggled in time with his pulse.

I retreated in terror, my stomach turning in horrified revulsion.

I had turned to him as a comforter, a father angel who now intended to rape me. He seized me by the back of my thigh, and I lost my footing and fell on the slippery floor. He fell, too, seesawed on his gut, lodged between my legs. He climbed up my body, foaming at the mouth in eagerness.

I went berserk—I bit and clawed and tore out chunks of skin, ripped tufts of gray hair from his half-bald head. I was choking on the onion stench of his breath, but I fought for my life like a feral cat. He got a hold of my wounded hand and twisted it to the floor.

He splayed my legs and forced all his weight on top of me.

I felt there was no longer an escape, and I thought of all the men I'd loved and wrapped my legs around and given my all.

My body wasted to the ice-cold floor and surrendered.

A sound broke from my throat and rose and rose and rose until it became a cutting wail that echoed interminably through the halls of the house. I had never heard a sound like that before. A tremor ran through me. I began to whimper.

He startled, snapped out of it. His fat face softened and his expression became that of the comforter once again. I caught a glimmer of fear in his bulging eyes. He wobbled to his feet and sat on the edge of the bathtub—gut and arse oozing down either side.

The sobbing started anew.

— Wha—what are you going to—are you going to d-d-o with me? I thought you were going to be good like a da-da-ddy.

Tears streamed down my cheeks.

He could hardly make out what I said, but he pursed his frothy lips and let a strange expression cross his face—a blubbery horseshoe formed around his mouth.

I pitied him something awful—so much so that I forgot my own misery.

He must have a daughter, maybe a girl about my age.

He sniffled, dejectedly twisting the diamond ring around his finger. I started to put my clothes on, and in my hurry, managed to tear my dress even more. Everywhere I went, I wreaked havoc. I came along like the devil made flesh and tempted this normally scrupulous man, this man who looked like one of Jesus' very apostles.

Hadn't he been good to me?

I ran out of the room, crept down the carpeted staircase. The front door slammed shut behind me and I sprinted away. I ran like a hunted deer, one street after another; in the piercing-cold wind, my tattered dress started to freeze where it had soaked up tears and wine. Snow bombarded my face.

I was bone-cold, and began to search for shelter.

All the buildings were closed shut. The storm rushed down every alley, howling.

Shivering, I pressed my face up against car windows, marveling at their upholstered seats and warm wool blankets. Every one of them was locked. Not knowing what else to do, I made my way toward the rear door of a little red car, and fiddled with the lock.

It popped right up.

Húrra! It was open.

I was absolutely dripping with joy at the discovery and I marveled at God's providence. I curled into a little ball on the backseat and wrapped my cloak around myself. I let drowsiness overtake me. A long time passed, and I believe I fell asleep. I woke with a start to the sound of a jackhammer. The day was bright and the sun had already started to shine. I was cold through and numb all the way up to my chest. I couldn't move and closed my eyes in hope of visions—until I heard footsteps outside. The door was flung open.

— Ma'am! Ma'am! May I ask what you are doing in my car?

I opened my eyes again.

The owner of the car was a stern-looking man in an expensive suit. He wasn't about to show me any compassion or clemency. I could see it from his gabardine overcoat.

— One has to sleep somewhere, I said, sitting up.

— Well, you can sleep somewhere else. My backseat isn't a bedroom. Clear out of here right now. Now, I said. You hear me? This car isn't parked here to house trash like you.

I dragged myself out and tried to climb onto my numb feet. I felt like I was dead up to my middle. I took a few steps, fell to the ground, and got back up. My feet dragged behind me, and I kept falling. But I managed to distance myself from the car and, more to the point, its owner.

I was on the west side of town, just up from the sea.

Snow-white seagulls wheeled circles in the air, while waves crested in long rows on cobalt stretches of ocean, up to the tide line. The sunlight was bright, and spans of pinkish clouds stretched above the glacier.

I breathed fresh air into my belly, and folded my hands at the beauty of it.

Somebody blew a drawn-out wolf whistle in my direction. I looked around. It was a construction worker in blue waterproofs and rubber boots.

— Hello, gorgeous. You had some fun last night, didn't you? He called.

I had just started to feel my feet again. Across from me was another laborer, dressed identically to the first, but in yellow. I suddenly found myself surrounded by workers.

I felt optimistic at the thought of good company, and intended to walk over to them, but collapsed on the pavement.

Somebody picked me up and carried me into a shed, sat me down next to a potbelly stove. They shoveled coal into the oven liberally and the heat warmed my face. I felt that I had frozen all the way up to my neck, and my unkempt hair hung over my eyes. I shook as the heat spread over me. An older man in a sealskin cap, with watering eyes and a drippy nose, stroked my hair. Then he pulled a dirty handkerchief from his pocket and dried my face. He smelled pleasantly of tobacco.

— She's got beautiful eyes, he said.

The young men at the table were remarkably loud, and cracked jokes at the foreman as if it were nothing. From time to time, they shot me shy glances.

— Don't you want coffee? One asked.

— Of course she wants coffee.

He reached for his thermos, poured coffee into a cup, and handed it to me. It was sugary and milky. Its radiant heat warmed my palms.

—She's probably hungry, too, one of the young men said. Light hair peeked out from underneath his black, knitted cap.

He pulled a snack wrapped in a rust brown package out of his pocket. He brought the slice of bread to my mouth. I bit into it. It was smeared with butter and lamb paté. It was pure delight.

By then I had stopped shaking. I felt health in my every nerve—I could sense my body with a lucid mind and submitted to the feeling of still being alive—of not having sunken into the tarpit like the poor little mice.

I finished the bread and drank the coffee I was offered—somebody handed me a cigarette, another lit it for me.

How extraordinary it was to exist. The men weren't put off—they didn't ask any questions; they just got me to my feet and helped me out.

They understood.

They smiled and waved goodbye. Somebody whistled a new dance song, and I heard the hum behind me. I had never so clearly understood how good people were to one another, and good to God, and how good God was to people and to himself.

I was bursting with a laughter of joy, of vitality.

The sun had begun to melt the snow on the south side of the houses, and little birds hopped in the puddles that remained, singing and gathering seeds that some good people had scattered beneath the kitchen windows.

Their songs and cheerful tittering filled me with indescribable gladness.

I had some trouble walking because the heels of my shoes felt loose and the pain in my marred and ragged feet was sharp, but I was well warm.

I had begun to hum a tune and to kick little, lovely stones out in front of me as I made my way down the street.

THE DREAM

I had a dream.

A dream that would take root; a rather rare course for a dream.

I waited in anticipation. It would happen on a sunny day in May—anything can happen on those days—or on a blue spring night, just as the morning strings itself across the sky in golden ropes.

It was a precious dream about a rare jewel, and I marvelled at having dreamt it.

I suspected that others would try to destroy the jewel, out of envy or malice, and I was on my guard so that nobody would get the chance. It was hidden away, but it was far from secure. Nothing can dissuade someone who means to steal, and precious things can also be lost, never to be found.

I kept this precious thing in an unusual place—inside of me—and I only half-knew where. It grew there, and its value grew, too, in its mystical way.

I had never seen them, but I knew what they would look like when they came into the light of day. They would have tiny hands, with pinkish nails, and feet that couldn't walk, so I would carry them in my arms.

Their gunmetal grey eyes would be so full of eyes that you could hardly see the whites; their translucent lenses would reflect the world in wordless questions. A dull copper sheen would flash through their light, wavy locks, and a spring breeze would eddy around their little ears. And I knew even more than that.

Little, white teeth would hide behind beautiful, red lips; they would sometimes cry and sometimes laugh. They would speak a remarkable language that nobody could understand a single word of, though it's spoken up in heaven, and everyone knows it before they come to Earth. They lose it almost immediately, if they end up staying.

These traits are to be treasured, that's for certain, and I was more than a little proud to carry such a wonder.

I didn't have them alone, of course—someone else had them with me—I didn't feel jealous. I felt none the worse. The two of us, who would cherish this precious creature, had gotten them for nothing, absolutely nothing.

It may be difficult to believe, but my co-owner wasn't happy about the news. The idea that such a dream would take root on a blue spring night, without warning, turned him cold. He wanted to tear the precious thing apart and out of me, so they would never make it into the light of spring in one piece. More to the point, he demanded that it be done immediately, as soon as possible, he said.

At first, I was shocked. But then it occurred to me that he didn't suspect how infinitely precious they were; never before had such a creature been formed, and never again would another like them live, not for all eternity.

I tried to help him to understand—you can't just destroy a thing like this, I said. They're irreplaceable; destroying them would be a wound to the world, to all beauty, goodness, and reason. The act would be a gash in the world's whole happiness. After I'd made this daring plea, I looked hopefully at him.

But he didn't want to understand, or maybe he couldn't.

And he became angry.

—There's enough of them in the world, and they're all damned to hardship, he hissed.

I protested. He got angrier. Then I reminded him he couldn't take my treasure from me.

– Then you'll be doomed along with it, you little fool! He burst out.

I began to cry, and he left me alone. I cried for a long time.

But then I righted myself, and I realized what a great responsibility it was to have such a precious thing alone— but that made my joy all the richer.

And I found it strange that, when people looked at my belly, they made such odd expressions. It didn't seem to gladden them, as I'd anticipated; instead, their faces filled with judgement and spite. It occurred to me that they might envy me, and so I took it lightly.

But when my friends began to avoid me—after side-eyeing my swollen stomach—I started to take it more seriously.

I couldn't understand. I took it quite personally, but I tried to forget.

I had very little money, so started to look for a job. It did not go well.

Employers looked probingly at my stomach and scanned my finger for a ring.

I looked back at their stomachs, too; they looked farther along than me. But they had rings on their fingers—many rings.

I looked them in the eyes, and I waited for them to look me in my eyes. But they never did. And I never found work.

An acquaintance, elderly and respectable, passed me in the street one autumn evening, when the trees flushed red and leaves eddied in a soft breeze.

I greeted her warmly.

She seemed not to hear me, shot me a sharp glance. That was the first time I had ever felt a pair of eyes bore through me.

– You aren't even ashamed, she said, and from her tone I understood that I should be ashamed.

– Do you think nothing of propriety, of decency? She barked, sizing me up. Do you really think we can't see what you've done? She strode off without saying goodbye and I stood stock-still, sore and stunned. Of course, she was referring to how my child came into being, it was plain as day.

I tried to recall whether I'd done something wicked.

I remembered his thick, coppery hair—how I had run my hands through it, buried my face in it, and drunk in his scent with an unquenchable thirst. I knew his sharp, white teeth, watched them fluoresce in the darkness above me; I searched for his moist, warm lips until I felt them close around mine…an untameable, burgeoning happiness surged through me when I wrapped my arms around his thin body and accepted him.

I shook from head to toe in fantastic anticipation and hungered for us to become one. I opened my legs to him.

I held him with this mad, ravenous self-love knew no bounds.

I couldn't find anything ugly in it; I loved remembering it, and I fantasized about it again and again.

But now my stomach turned; I felt completely alone. I had nobody to nestle up to, no hand to hold.

I felt myself sink into an unspeakable sadness at the thought that he would be gone, that I would never get to wrap myself around him. I wanted, when I reminded myself of how things had been, to die.

People called after me in the street when I wandered outside, drunk.

When I looked around, my heart fluttered at the prospect of running into friends, but these faces were all unknown to me. They looked at me without the least mercy, and their eyes felt like thrusts of the spear. They burst into disdainful, rollicking laughter.

Inside me, I felt a stab of pain, but I tried to make the best of my situation; I smiled, mortified. I racked my brains over it, over and over and over it: Why had they mocked me.

Did my hair make them feel so resentful? My eyes?

Did they know I was carrying a child? I'd often wondered why people looked at my stomach with scorn.

I didn't know how to beg their forgiveness for my existence; or for throwing myself into the arms of a gorgeous man without hesitation; or for drinking and smoking in the merriment of a moment; or for enjoying life to the fullest, for being happier than they suspected, for containing the most precious dream in the world without their permission.

I wanted more than anything to earn their absolution.

They could take everything from me if I could just walk in the streets undisturbed.

I wasn't going to take anything from them, nothing, absolutely nothing though I had dreamed this dream of spring and everything then unfolding.

I dreamt.

A saucer in front of me with a blue rim and a cup without handles, filled with cold water.

On the saucer, three boiled red potatoes, round and steaming. I was hungry and hurried to slice one in half. In its centre, a purple ring shimmered in the starch of the wound.

My mouth began to water. I was just about to devour them, devour all of them, when a small child reached its hands up over the edge of the table, reaching for the potatoes.

They were my child, the precious being I'd never set eyes upon. I had no doubt.

Their light hair had a dull copper sheen, and their gunmetal grey eyes were so full of eyes that you could hardly see the whites. I read their wordless questions, reached for their other little hand and placed it on my knee, feeling bashful—as one always does around unfamiliar children.

To disguise my shyness, I began to peel the potatoes.

The child grabbed one with both hands, but it was too hot to lift.

I mashed the potatoes with my fork and blew on them to cool them. Then I took a tiny morsel and raised it to their little mouth.

But just then, a hand reached past my shoulder and snatched the saucer away.

The child began to cry, in the bitter, angry way that little children do when they've been bullied by adults and have no way to avenge themselves.

I tried, unsuccessfully, to quiet the child because I felt certain the culprit was divine. It's not nice when children make a racket when guests come calling, much less god. I couldn't understand what god intended to do with the potatoes, but I felt a belligerent need to rebel against him, as I sometimes did with people who slung abuses at me.

And although I guessed I was fighting an uphill battle, I decided I would get these fantastic potatoes for better or worse. I turned hard on my heel.

– I want my potatoes, I said.

The being was draped in green, with a white veil across its face.

I was puzzled by god's goofy costume and, also, why he wasn't bigger.

– These are not your potatoes, the being said. They belong to others.

– Okay, but I need them, the kid needs them, I snapped.

– Thou shalt not steal, the being said ceremoniously.

– But it's so little, it makes no difference to anyone, I said.

– You still can't have them, the being said coldly.

I took another tack. God might be merciful if approached in the right way.

– Hey, god. I heard that you're charitable, I said, gently.

– God helps those who help themselves, the being answered in turn.

– But the child is so hungry. Good people have to give a hungry kid potatoes.

– Good people, he boomed. Then good people would end up doling out potatoes to poor children for all eternity!

I didn't give up. God's stony heart would soon melt.

– But just this once, I pleaded. Can't you hear how the child is crying? Just give us the potatoes this once, just this one time – this single, solitary time! Do this for us, good lord.

And I reached out my hand for the saucer.

– God is righteous, the being answered severely, getting ready to leave.

I was furious. So that's how he wanted it. To make me beg, even as my child cried with hunger pains, while he made off with the potatoes.

I was made stronger by hatred.

God had finally met his match—and he wasn't a real big man—even though he thought himself almighty!

My little child would be fed. I had not a doubt in my mind.

I grabbed the hand that held onto the potato dish and squeezed it with all my might. I felt how the bones crowded together under the pressure of my grip, and the dish crashed to the stone floor with a bang; the succulent mash squished into the cracks and squashed into a stinking ooze.

The child's loud, violent cry magnified my anger, oil thrown on a fire.

– I'll kill you! I screamed, twisting the creature's arm with all the force I could muster. It was then that I noticed its hand had long, lacquered nails. Red nails.

I jolted.

So it was the devil! It had to be the devil! The fiend! God could hardly be so ghoulish—I should have worked it out right away. I trembled with thoughts of mutiny, of getting the upper hand against the devil.

I, of all people, had the chance to give him his just deserts, and it wouldn't go unseized. For the blink of an eye I forgot how bad people had been to me, how they went out of their way to hurt me and torment me, how they denied me everything with such ferocity—they denied me even the tiniest understanding, and pierced me with their eyes—and now I had to defend the rights of the people, avenging all the injustice the devil had ever or would ever engineer.

Avenge it memorably – here and now!

And all at once, I realized that people weren't bad in and of themselves, that the devil made them that way.

No, people were good. It was the fiend who was bad. The fiend alone!

But the being exploited my moment's hesitation to liberate itself. It backed away.

– Are you really going to behave like this—toward me? It asked gently, though vexed. It turned to the child, who was tuckered out from crying.

I thought it intended to stroke my child's blonde hair, and I resented it: I didn't want the devil to cosy up to my gem, my artifact from paradise.

But then, right before my eyes, its long, red-lacquered claws locked around the child's head and ripped each hair at the root, as nimbly as a maid might pluck a chicken. It was disgusting, indescribable. Light, iridescent copper locks clumped into bloody daggers.

The child released a cry that resonated in my bones.

I meant to rush toward them, to save them, but I could move neither stem nor stern. I knew the being would tear the child apart right in front of my eyes, and in the stupor of fear and hatred, I tried to recall something I knew existed, and the one thing that could help me—just one word!

I gasped and watched the creature push its blue-red index finger, sharp as an arrowhead, into the child's eyes, into those deep, gunmetal grey eyes which in my dreams were mirrors of the greatest beauty in the world. The creature pried them out, leaving only large holes, gaping, bloody, full of red darkness.

With a kind of wildness akin to madness, I tried to recall that one word—the magic word that would save everything, free us from this suffering...

Through the slits of my eyelids, I could still see how it tore the child apart, slowly, slowly, limb from limb—that little, lovely body I had loved so dearly, that should have danced on the green earth in the spring light, as in that beautiful premonition.

Time whirled away from me and I couldn't remember the magic word; I couldn't make the miracle—not yet!

Eternities passed. The child's wailing died once and for all. The little body lay dismembered in the mud, slick red blood ran together with silty water.

Beauty's mirror had been broken, and would never be whole again, it would never again reflect this splendor, never!

The world had had lost its jewel and would never find it again.

The child's like had never existed, would never exist again for all of eternity!

I couldn't cry, I couldn't move, I couldn't breathe, I couldn't make a sound.

The creature tidily removed its veil and took care to dry its hands with the cloth.

Then it looked me straight in the eyes, and smiled.

I jumped, as if from electric shock, and I felt my heart stop.

That smile, that horrifying, calculated, malicious smile—so endlessly animal, selfish, lustful!

How well I knew it: the green satin dress, the long red nails, the puckered lips, a mouth that blended the simpleton smile of the lord and the deceitful smirk of the devil. The smile in the mirror!

Me.

Then I remembered the magic word, as if lit by lightning—the word that could have undone the event in progress; transformed the past into nothing—but it was too late: Wake up!

I was long awake.

The street was a rushing sea of people, and though I could hardly walk, I carried myself forward without direction.

I heard the hum of activity around me as if through a partition, and I thought I was dead. I couldn't remember where I was going, or why, but I wanted so much to sleep, even though there was nowhere to rest but the ground.

Then somebody called my name, and I was so glad I stopped still.

In this enormous sea of strange faces, I had one friend, one person willing to recognize me, who would help me out of the street—maybe they'd promise to hold my hand while I slept.

Who could it be? I looked around excitedly. But I only saw faces I'd never seen before, though I knew their expression—scornful, hateful faces filled with devilish gladness at having played me. Faces with eyes that stared at my abdomen without mercy and fed on the shame that ran red to my cheeks as a raptor would feed on blood.

A lump formed in my throat, and tears filled my eyes, but I raised my quivering hand and waved warmly.

Would they really continue to hate me? Didn't they know there was nothing to gain from ostracizing me any longer, that the child had been taken out of me, that it was dead—that its little, beautiful body had been hideously dismembered and left in a black dumpster?

Didn't they know I had nothing more than they did—now I was poorer than the poorest of all? Didn't they know I had endured terrible pain for the happiness that I'd dared to enjoy, the happiness I'd stolen from those who could never enjoy it?

I had been punished and I had asked for forgiveness and now I would stand humbled before them and beg rich women for a home and fat men for work and sage men for guidance. But I read the stern denial in all their eyes, even before I offered up my plea.

I had hoped they would forgive my transgressions when my swollen belly returned to normal, that they would forget I had ever had the beautiful dream. I now saw I was mistaken.

I would never be forgiven.

A few men in expensive suits called after me. They'd seen the blood puddled on the back of my dress.

The words echoed in my head long after their contribution had died out: Harlot! Don't you want to change your clothes?

I, unfortunately, had nothing else to wear. I staggered cautiously past a group of young girls who were tending a flowerbed on the lawn.

I tried to hold my dress tight to myself to hide the blood—my coat was too short to conceal it.

Streams of blood began to run down my thighs, thick and hot, down my bare legs and into my shoes.

I knew that I needed to sit down somewhere if I didn't want it to show.

I collapsed against a corrugated fencing around the lawn, sank down to my knees, and rested my face against it.

I was alone. Alone. And nobody was willing to recognize me, nobody in the entire world.

The dream had been destroyed—it would never take root, not even on a blue spring night—not even when the morning climbed a golden rope into a vernal window.

My child was dead, I couldn't forget, my lover hated me, never again would I wish to die from pleasure in his arms, never, but I wanted to be dead now, to be dead here against the ice-cold iron.

I couldn't contain my sobs, couldn't control them.

The young girls by the flower bed screeched cackles. They burst into laughter when somebody had cracked a good joke:

— I bet you've heard a whore curse. But have you ever heard one pray?

The joke was followed by a swell of laughter.

Incidentally, I had forgotten to pray. I closed my eyes and tried to recite a short prayer, but it broke apart into spasmodic sobs.

THE MAN AND HIS HOUSE

– I wonder if I'll end up dying here? The man asked himself. He was re-arranging his things inside the portable cabin that had become his home.

The house sat on a round bay with a northwesterly mouth; the caerulean sea was embroidered with the white crests of waves. Circling seagulls overhead, likewise, were white, but only from his perspective on the ground: from above, their backs and the tips of their wings were a darker shade of gray.

– Where do all these fowl go? He asked himself. A skein of ducks glided past; the din of their incessant calling hammered in his ears like the engine thrum of motor boats. The birds put a great deal of work into flying, as did the eiders, and all birds of that sort, for that matter.

The man stepped away from his task after a while to contemplate the birds. He knew the gulls well; he knew where the effortless, even careless, flaps of their wings would lead them—where and to what. Though he had lived with them for three years, he felt that he hardly knew the ducks. Looking after them was a futile exercise, but it was nevertheless his.

– Maybe they're getting some exercise, he said to the air. Then he remembered that it was still high summer; there were yet unfledged ducklings in the pond.

– Oh, who knows where they're going.

He resumed his work. He had been gathering no-good objects into no-good boxes that he stacked one on top of another. It seemed a trivial occupation, but the man was securing fuel. No two people gather fuel in the same way.

It was a cloudy day, though not sunless, and well past nine o'clock in the morning, so-called dagmál. Rain hung in the sky to the north. The man's house was engulfed by mayweed and chickweed and tufted grasses in greens and whites; rusted iron poked up out of the scrubby brush, which was strewn with broken glass, wood scraps. His plot had once been a garbage dump, now disused for some time.

To the south, his home looked out over a green, reedy pond occupied by a blizzard-white swan, a few ducks. A man with better vision would have noticed another whooper swan, too, in a nest at the far end of the pond. Anyone who lived in the countryside should be aware of duck and eider nests in these reedy stretches, all the way up to the moor. Birds out here on the fringes of the city spook far more easily than those near its center.

The rain came on. The drops fell slowly, hardly perceptible, but the man could hear them breaking on the corrugated iron roof and watched them dapple the light wood of his crates, which had been bleached by sea. He threw a torn sailcloth over the pile and touted.

– I wonder if I'm going to die here? He repeated, his thoughts elsewhere, his eyes turned westward.

Dark clouds drifted toward him, despite the calm windlessness around him on the ground.

– It's gunna start blowin' from the west tunight, the man said. A westerly wind. It'll dry off tomorrow, maybe around noon.

He pressed his lips together. He knew better than to predict auspicious weather aloud. As soon as it heard, it changed its plans. He's good at bailing himself out.

– Oh, now then. Summer isn't yet over. I can gather enough today to burn… if they don't take the shack from me after all, he said.

"They" were unpredictable. Bjarni had told him without hesitation that he could leave his cabin put, provided construction hadn't begun. But what was the story the last time? Bjarni had said: The construction's going to start, old friend! And he'd had to move his cabin over to the dump. They'd begun to pave, and even finished a few certain areas. But three years had passed, and nothing more had been done. The weeds and grasses that surrounded his cabin by the dump were overgrown. Even the flies given up the ghost.

Yet in summer, the wind changed: They're going to start construction soon, Bjarni had said. You've got to go, my good man. We're making plans.

And he had started to prepare himself. He fretted. But then an unexpected gift came to his aid: A few spoiled teenagers, sons of Independecers, made regular visits to the junkyard road around noon, which was more or less when they roused and got to their feet. They tried to shock themselves awake with washy gin and cokes in their mother's car. And they had weapons. A car full of expensive rifles and shot guns and handguns, and they made quite a lot of noise with them.

They hardly ever hit their target, though their guns were expensive and well-made. But they did damage. Birds bolted from their nests. One of the boys—he had been in the Shooting Club—killed two flightless old drakes and one lame eider.

Their lifeless bodies circulated in the pond, where the boys couldn't have reached them anyway even if they'd tried. As the man waited for a southerly breeze to carry the carcasses to the shore, he swore to give them a talking to next time.

The next day, it was a stroke of luck that Guðbrandur had come. Guðbrandur was the director of the Bird Preservation Society and was looking into a few swans that had flown the city pond. He had shown Guðbrandur the corpses and could prove his story as soon as the young men came back. Guðbrandur had told him: Everything is in order, old man, if you watch over the birds, especially the swans, I will make sure you can stay here as long as you like.

And the man had harangued the emerging pillars of society until they took to shooting elsewhere during nesting season; or, at least, the same boys never came twice. From then on, he'd seen the boys in that pink and white Kaiser drinking their gin and cokes around noon, but they never carried Remington rifles, or double-barreled shotguns, or even revolvers. Though you could hear the American military's radio station blasting from the car, the sound of gunshots quieted, and the birds settled once again. Their young flourished around the reedy pond—not only ducks and eider, but also whopping, grayish yellow swanlings.

The more responsible and well-raised young men in the area believed he was a real ranger, a ranger from the park service, or the government, and that the cabin was his outpost.

They'd believed he was on the payroll of the public, no less. Had they suspected that he lived there—and that it was his home, and that he had nowhere else to go—it would have been an altogether different matter.

But some still harassed him, even though they didn't know he wasn't a servant of the state. They threatened him with the Ministry of Foreign Affairs and their pabbis and the Ministry of Ecclesiastical Affairs and some sort of defense alliance—they even threatened to beat him to a pulp during his shift. He knew he could handle two or three teenagers, even though they had rich, butter bones. But his bones were of winter wheat and had grown hard from harsh weather. He just scoffed at them.

Had they known this was his one and only home, they would have burnt it down around him. He was sure of that.

And even though Guðbrandur had said he would make sure the cabin stayed put, he wasn't altogether confident. Because Bjarni and the Administrative Committee of the Administration had so much more power than Guðbrandur and the Bird Protection Society, even though the birds were as many as the principles behind them.

What power could one little group of idealists wield against an entire Administrative Committee? None.

They had no more influence than a flicker of feeling over steely logic.

He had started to think so warmly of this cabin and this place and this pond and these birds. His entire life, he had tried not to feel warmth toward anything. It had gone better than he'd expected. For instance, since his first time, he'd been able to see women for what they were. Except maybe Soffia. Two years of nights had passed without her, and she'd taken up with another man and married him. That's what she'd done.

Yes, he'd been led so far along he'd even started to think about things like dependable income and a little basement apartment.

But those days were behind him, and it was for the best. He had started to take a shining to this hovel, in their absence. The pond with its ducks, so shy nobody would ever really know them. And this hissing swan couple and their four young.

But they were no better than Soffia. They would leave in the autumn, too, just like her. Maybe they'd vanish altogether.

It was painful to think about. He lumbered toward the entrance to the cabin, focusing his thoughts on his coffee.

He'd felt so stately when the cupboard was first brought inside. Having something to fill meant something to him. And he thought of the little pink curtains in front of the window—yes, it was over, but she was still there.

He was getting old, too; he had had long wallowed in self-pity and thought often of death. This was the most often he'd thought about death since he'd first heard about it as a child.

He recalled, still uncomfortably, the first time the fair one had visited him at night. How her mane of white gold, dripping wet, reached all the way to the floor as she sat on his bed, her blue-green dress bunched up around her thin body.

She had only appeared before great sickness, hardship— or a big move. She had lived here in the bay, and she had followed him when he moved kilometers down shore.

He wasn't necessarily afraid of her. He had often dreamed of her, but she had never come to him in waking except to warn him of something. Soffía had driven her away, except on that first night. And on the last night, she grinned at them from the doorway.

She knew, she knew what he didn't know. She was his companion in her malignant, ugly way.

He sat down on a stone near the front door but had forgotten his coffee. The rain fell quietly, calmly on his gray hair and his purplish, bloated hands, which he rested on the timeworn, torn knees of his trousers.

When he died, how much time would pass before somebody would find him? He joked cynically to the air.

Yes, who? And how long would it take?

Couldn't be long. Dóri the Book would come. And Beggi. And Úndína, Sylvía, and Dása. But it would still take at least ten days, maybe more, before a body came looking.

He hoped that it was a woman if a long time passed. They could do with the stench and rot of the dead, handling the slack corpse that they'd rolled with in the hay in better days.

He coughed a dry, loud laugh.

135

He'd often told them to make the most of the night. He wouldn't leave behind his thing when he left.

And they'd agreed with him.

It was decidedly modest, this so-called poor man's sport, but he had tried to spice it up.

On the other hand, maybe it'd be Dóri the Book. If it were him, he hoped beyond hope that he'd get a chance to leave a fiver under the Book of Psalms by the coffee canister—the porcelain one from Soffía.

Dóri the Book had always brought him things—most often food, but sometimes firewater or wood spirits. Dóri the Book had to have a reason to come by. When had Dóri the Book ever sat down for a drink without running some errands for him first?

Maybe it would be Beggi. If it were Beggi, then he'd leave a glass of wood spirits behind the corner of the bed next to the brown chest. Beggi thought wood spirits were better than any other drink. Beggi knew where he kept it. And Beggi never paid any mind to gin, whisky, or his stiffening arteries, if wood spirits were to be had.

Everyone has their poor man's sport. Even the poorest needed something to delight in, however insignificant.

But what was his?

Not alcohol—that was one way to pass the time, but something he could well do without.

Not the company of others—he had long ago laid those oars down. He didn't need other people—not even Dóri the Book, who was so willing to run errands.

He could well go himself.

And it wasn't women; they might come along, pitiful as they were, but he didn't need them. Not even Dása, who was so wild in bed.

That was all a part of another world, another happiness that didn't concern him.

Didn't he have anything to be happy about then? Didn't he have joy to carry around like the others?

Yes, he had his own happiness. When he had worked enough for a portion of salted meat and parcel of salted cod, a box full of coal and enough dried firewood from the dump, he'd relish climbing into his shabby bed and listening to autumn rain reverberating on the roof. He'd open an old album with buck-naked photos of women he'd clipped from magazines. He'd savor the sound of embers cooling in the coal stove, safe in the knowledge that their warmth would last through the night, that the pond would be deserted until next spring, and that the snow outside would thaw to reveal mayweed and dock rosettes.

He had certainly gotten old, but he loved this place. He rose from his stone reluctantly and shook himself off.

Blessed coffee. Blessed old cabin.

– I wonder if I'll get to die here? He asked the indifferent late summer rain.

THE STREET IN THE RAIN

The evening sun cast a glow over the wet pavement, its reflections in the puddles threw luminescent spears in all directions. Raindrops fluttered toward the ground like dying moths drinking in light as they fell nearer and nearer to the earth.

A seawind rushed through the trees, stroked the grass, lifted laundry hanging on feeble lines.

My dress was soaked through and had glued itself to me. I felt the brunt of the cold as it struck my bare legs like a sail drenched by the surf. But the rain had begun to let up, and my clothes would soon dry. That sat well with me.

I felt thirsty and a little hungry, but what I really craved was the cigarette I did not have.

And so when a welcoming bench beckoned me over, I heaved myself onto it, exhausted.

That bench was my ticket. It opened the world before me, as if I were seated in a big theater without having to pay the price of admission, considering the stage dressing.

At gloaming, the white and ochre gables of the houses took on the appearance of unwritten pages, their rooves casting a thousand iridescent sheens of green, black, and red.

The characters trod the graphite asphalt. Young men, straight-backed and bold, strutted past me, bantering in booming voices. Young women walked arm in arm, whispering to one another before breaking into shrieking peals of laughter as sharp as glass shards.

Across the street, a child cried over its wrecked car. The tears spilled just as quickly as he could dry them.

An old woman with swollen hands, eyes downcast, pushed a rubbish bin into a port.

Then, just beside me, two doves were playing. The globes of their dark eyes burned, and they cooed, smitten, fluttering their white wings, and gently lifting off from the cement gutters. Their movements scattered raindrops like cinders.

As this scene unfolded, an old drunk staggered up the road and walked over to me. He held out his shaking, bone-bare hand, and sat down heavily on the bench.

– You should be happy, he said in a chiding voice. – Tonight, the wind is blowing to the north. Why are you crying?

I looked up and stroked my cheeks with my handkerchief.

– I'm not crying, I said. The sun is just in my eyes.

He pulled out a bottle of black death and lifted it to the light. It was just under half empty.

– It's death, he said, a little arrogantly. Want some?

A little pick-me-up is never a bad thing, so without answering, I accepted the bottle and took a good gulp. It was straight, undiluted and unblended, and I immediately felt a little sick. But then a wave of warmth traveled through me. The drunk gave me a look.

– I think you need a cigarette to go with that, he said.

He took out two rolled cigarettes from his breast pocket and handed me one. I lit it, having stopped shaking for the most part. More of the cold left my body. The day's beauty began its ascent to a higher order, nearing perfection. The drunk began to sing a psalm to himself but lost the melody and stopped.

– Lissen, you gotta fiver? He rasped.

My cheeks turned a deep scarlet. I didn't have a cent to spare for this generous man.

To conceal my embarrassment, I dug in my empty pockets, even though I knew there was nothing to find.

– No, I don't, I whispered. – It's all gone.

The drunk looked at me compassionately:

– It's no matter. I only wanted to get some soup, hot soup. There's a girl who sells me soup sometimes when I'm hungry.

He looked at me as if he were begging my forgiveness.

– I don't often have enough for food, he added.

He took a big gulp from the bottle and lurched into a coughing fit.

I thought he would never catch his breath. I supported him while he writhed, as the cough ripped him apart, pulled him back together.

143

His cigarette dropped into a puddle, and its little ember died out with a hiss and the dry tobacco drank in the water as if it were a sponge.

His drink ran out of the sides of his mouth, down his dirty beard, his neck. I stroked his cheeks with my palm and dried his face with the rag of my handkerchief. I handed him the other cigarette once he'd righted himself.

And downed another sip from the bottle. Skál! I said.

He looked up, surpised.

– Now you're jolly, he said. That's how girls should be when the sun shines—young girls, happy girls. Cheers!

His beard curved into a broad smile across his sullen face, and I noticed that he was missing his entire upper row of teeth.

– Can I tell you something? He asked. Once upon a time, I sat on a bench with a girl in a beautiful garden— years ago. It was a young girl, as beautiful as you, and she was good to me, too, just like you. I think I remember it right – drizzling like now, with happy sunlight in between the showers.

The drunk fell silent and stared beyond me for a long while.

I looked into his eyes, threaded with blood, as some mysterious well filled them to the brim.

He didn't move his head, his smile didn't falter. The tears began to fall like trails of quicksilver onto his shabby clothing, joining the rivers of rain that ran into the puddles.

I shook my hair out of my face.

– Did she die? I asked.

The drunk came to his senses. He had started to sob.

– No, she's still al-li-live. Shepard, Shepard's purse grows over her no-now.

I handed him my handkerchief and he dried his face. Then he looked straight into my eyes.

– Li-listen. I've heard you can write. C-could you write a little something for her – even something modern, a poem. P-please.

He looked at me hopefully. The sobs had slowed.

– I'll try, I said. Cheers! Cheers to the sunshine. Don't you find it strange, rain in the sunshine?

The drunk took a glug from the bottle and measured the remaining liquid using the light. Then he looked at me, smiling.

– That means it'll stop raining, he said. It'll start blowing from the north tonight. Then, quietly, he added: The bottle's almost empty.

– Don't you think it'll get cold? I asked, feeling something between hope and fear.

– No, no. Not in high summer, except sometimes around sunrise. And you heat up quickly when it rises…

Our cigarette had now gone out, and the drink was done.

The drunk handed the other stub to me.

– Remember to write the memorial, he said. Add something about mayweed. I'm going down to Stræti[1].

– Sure, I said, shelving the stub in my bra. I hope you get some soup.

145

He stumbled down the street, singing:

Jesus wants me for a sunbeam,
To shine for Him each day;
In every way try to please Him,
At home, at school, at play.

His quivering, husky voice choked into a violent cough, and he fell to his knees. The empty bottle struck the pavement and shattered into smithereens, startling the white doves.

They flew off, sailing over green eaves.

The drunk got to his feet, wiped his bloody hand on his jacket. He'd cut himself on the shards. Then off he went, bowling down the street.

The breeze carried a scrap of song to me:

Jesus wants me for a sunbeam,
To shine for Him each day

I settled into the ecstacy of the booze, of my vacant mind, of the heavy touch of each drop of rain.

A certain calm—a restful numbness—washed over me. I heard the song of a big band playing on rain gutters, the lids of garbage cans. The rain's singing, falling scale harmonized in speed and step with a piano solo played by the genius composer. This grand orchestra. A rising, searching staccato. The rain swelled, beating the drums, the drumsticks hissed a roll on the corrugated iron rooves.

I was blissful. I felt neither hunger nor cold, and still had half a cigarette. What did it matter that I was a little thirsty and didn't have any matches? It was wonderful to be alive.

I began to think about the memorial. My mood lifted higher and higher.

I wanted to dwell here forever and a day.

The orchestra continued its symphony.

– Good afternoon!

The address was so aggressive I jumped. It was the police. They'd sidled up to me, one on each side, stiff, cocky and as serious as their station, their hands behind their backs.

It was so suddenly, sadly quiet.

The orchestra stopped playing, as if its tape had been cut, and the raindrops pinged randomly on the lids of trash cans.

I used all my might to focus my thoughts. It was a pity that everyone was so good to me when I didn't need it.

A pity—plain and simple.

I only half-knew how to excuse myself:

– Thank you both very much, but god is already doing quite enough for me, and the police could hardly do better.

I had phrased it quite rudely, and I realized as much.

The policemen were a bit more tactful:

– But you're soaked, one of them said. Don't you want shelter?

Shelter! I pulled my knees into my chest, shaking at the memory of that claustrophobic cell, a tin can with tepid water. I winced at the thought, the thought of staying alone in the dark, cut off from the glory outside by iron bolts and stone walls; the thought of listening to the furious and fraught abuses of prisoners, wings pinioned in place, rather than the loving coos of white doves, the sunbeam songs of free men, the heavenly piano solo played on bin lids.

I forced as much vitality as I could into my smile to reinforce my position:

– Thank you very much, but that won't be necessary. It's god's way. When he showers on a person, he dries them after. The wind will start blowing from the north—the sunshine between the showers means the rain'll soon stop.

I took courage as I waited for them to drop the matter— thoughtful commentary on the weather is a surefire way to lighten the mood.

The policemen shot each other puzzled glances. Finally, one said:

– She's not that drunk. Best to leave her.

– Bye! I chirped, as if we were old chums. I walked out into the street with a bounce in my step, though I was trying hard to keep myself from staggering.

The white doves came back. They fluttered around me in a wide circle.

I was quite tired, and so unsteady on my feet that even the street tried its best to tempt me to sit down. An enticing patch of grass was just ahead and I propelled myself toward it with the last of my strength.

Even before I touched it, I could feel how soft it was. The tangy smell of earth swept over my senses.

But in the very last leg, my legs faltered—and I sank down gratefully into the fragrant, wet ground.

I fumbled for my cigarette until I remembered I didn't have matches.

The stub was dry now, and I carefully placed it back in my bra, happy to hold onto it.

I nestled into the earth and felt the wind still.

It started to rain again.

First, a few shy, scattered drops. Green clouds drew gauze over the sun, as the smattering thickened.

The immortal genius tried to play his instrument once more. It sounded like someone was drumming on hollow metal with the tips of their fingers.

Then the rain began to pour, and the drops struck the pavement like hail. I buried my head under my arms and felt the water seep into my clothes and stream down my hide.

Two young men had stopped on the sidewalk nearby.

– This one's schnockered, one said. Who's she?

– What, you don't know? It's the poet. Come on now, let's get out of here.

The sound of their footsteps grew faint and disappeared.

A little later, I heard them turn back. One stopped right beside me.

– We should help her. Otherwise, she'll be lying here all night.

– Hey, where do you live?

I looked up. The man was gorgeous—well-dressed and stylish—and eminently aware of it. He seemed to have better things to do than busy himself with a drunk girl in the street.

I thought it would be a disaster if his kindness didn't find an outlet.

– I have . . . I don't have a home, I said.

That struck him.

– What are you saying—you don't have a room?

– No, I said.

The young man seemed embarrassed by my answer.

– Don't you want to go inside somewhere? He asked. You'll be drenched.

– The earth is so warm, I said by way of excuse. I can't leave it.

A group of men gathered in the street. They all wanted to help me.

The young man didn't give up just yet.

– It's better if you can find some shelter, he said.

– Yes, but I don't have any place like that, I said. That's for other people.

The group formed a huddle.

Some wanted to take me to the police station. I prayed to god they wouldn't put me in that dark cell.

One suggested they take me home, but when it came to it, nobody could commit.

The young man came all the way out onto the lawn. He was so kind and helpful that it burned my heart.

– What can I do for you? He asked.

– Nobody can do anything for me, I said, heartsore.

Then it occured to me. I raised up on my elbows, releasing a long sigh of relief.

Something good could still come out of this.

– Do you have a match?

And I reached into my bra for my cigarette.

When I looked up, he was holding a full box of matches in the palm of his hand and another little cardboard pack, brimful of the best cigarettes in the world.

The Wellington stub from the old, toothless drunk suddenly lost its allure.

– Do you have a cigarette? This gorgeous man asked, handing me a bright white, smooth cigarette, as magical as a mysterious cog in a clock. It sent stabs to my heart when a ruthless raindrop fell on it.

It occurred to me that I could stash this one away with the other, but by then the young man had already lit the cigarette between my lips. The fragrant smoke seeped into my skin.

Out in the street, the others were quarrelling over who would save me, but they couldn't come to an agreement.

The rain continued to fall, but soundlessly, and I wondered at humankind's innate goodness. This group had convened under the floodgates of heaven on my account.

They hushed.

– Isn't it better to let her take care of herself? Someone said. People like that always find a way to survive.

Hush.

It seems like the best solution.

God interceded on behalf of the last speaker. Just as the man spoke, the downpour halted.

The wind pushed aside the greenish yellow curtains of the clouds and the sun burst through.

The young man smiled broadly and strode away from the lawn. The group whooped cheerful goodbyes. The men's doubts were swept away.

The big problem was solved. God had switched off the spout.

I stood up, stretched out, and wiped the droplets from my face.

The sun cast its red fire over the poison-green grass. Its brightness in my eyes turned the asphalt cobalt.

The cigarette gleamed white between my fingers and its blue smoke wound into the air joyfully, a prayer that's going to be heard.

1 Stræti, in this case, refers to Bar Reykjavík formerly on Hafnarstræti 15. According to critic Egill Helgason, "Hafnarstræti was the domain of róni." This term refers to alcoholic or chronic, often unhoused, drinkers. "From the pre-war years through 1960… if anybody lost their footing in life, they were said to have "gone to stræti. […] The Bar came to be associated with chronic drinkers."

THE WINDBREAK

The countryside is a completely different world. The atmosphere is different, the people are different, their hopes and needs are different.

There, because nature is wild and untamed, everything is entirely unlike city life. The land isn't unplanned but for small plots.

The animals live wild, free: Seals, fish, birds—mallards, swans, black-backed gulls, ravens, skua, merlins, eagles, all manner of heathland bird. The red-necked wader writes in ditches and peat trenches, the whimbrel titters short whistles when summer has fully and completely arrived—and the snipe sings auspices for lonely children left destitute.

On bright spring days, the sea is the blue of light inside a sapphire, or white like milk, and as the sun goes down, the mountains glow like molten embers.

The rivers' channels are as still and calm as deep lakes. Silver salmon rise to the surface to rest as they prepare for the approaching battle up the falls, even as seatrout with their iridescent rosy gold scales rush through streams in search of their purpose in life—which some find, and some don't.

Across the hills and moors, spring's big band plays its sublime symphony. The bandstand, the hills and cliffs, glint like wet scoria after a vernal downpour.

The white heads of cotton grass bob in the mire. In the hills, wishing stones shine in the sun between showers. Onyx sand is a black satin gown, lustrous on a proud and elegant woman.

It's no lie. It's a holy truth that few have witnessed, and thus only few believe.

But country children have seen it, and they do not doubt. Perhaps they're even happiest of all when the golden plover begins its refrain of *the glory, the glory*—and builds its nest in rubble rock by outcrops of golden dryads. Everyone wants to build their home in the most beautiful place in the wild kingdom. All children—orphans and stepchildren, rich and poor, behaved and naughty, little and big—brighten.

Rich children play as they like, wherever they like; they're permitted because they have so little work to do.

Poor children, who need to help mamma and pabbi, try to make a game of their work. In spring, even the most demanding tasks can become great amusements.

And then there are little motherless children that nobody loves. They might live with people they aren't related to, who think only of the money they're given for the orphan's tattered clothes and poor food. These hapless children have nobody to love them—nobody to comfort them when they cry, to stroke their wet cheek, to comb the tangles from their hair or warm their little hands when they're numb from the cold. They go off somewhere and whimper and soothe themselves, or they wander off in search of peace, though they're wretched and their feet are wet.

It's a relief to flee, to weep alone where nobody will spank or scold you.

When they sneak out on research expeditions in spring's majesty, they forget how cold their hands are, how water floods their thin sheepskin shoes.

They can forget all the bad.

The oystercatcher is black with red feet. Its call is a strange *plip-plip*. The redshank is grey and has a loud twang. The ring-necked plover is small, its plumage is striking, and it can sprint faster than all the other birds.

There's a lot for poor little children to see in the heath and at the sea.

There are shells, pretty stones, and mussels. And many strange things, too: profuse barnacles on seaside boulders, snails and tiny shrimp under pebbles.

And though most things are off-limits to a miserable four-year-old girl without parents, curiosity and the pursuit of truth run stronger in her than any fear or terror.

She set off, determined.

A four-year old has many things they need to explore. Even though a storm was blowing in from the north, and she was wearing poor and tattered protective clothing, and her sheepskin shoes were threadbare at the seams, and though her rough-spun socks were ragged and ratty, she didn't mind trudging through the marsh in the moorland.

She did not think of the cold of her hands, but her feet smarted from the coldshock of the puddles.

The whimbrel shot her a reproving glance out of the corner of its eye but continued to deliver a liturgy to its heart's content.

The girl suspected there was a plover nest in the hills above her and headed toward it straightaway.

Finding a plover's nest is one of the great wonders of the world—it's no surprise that the child's steps were drawn toward it. When she reached the top of the hill, her socks and shoes were wet through. She forgot all about the cold and the pain in her feet from the puddles when she neared tufts of mountain avens. The brown heads of dryads gone to seed tossed in the northern breeze, even as the yellow yolks of young blooms widened her eyes.

There, she'd seen a plover couple.

Although she intended to find the nest, much else could draw her attention.

The redshank and the oystercatcher crowded the air with an astonishing din, as if they were trying to start a pop band.

But even they were nothing compared to the arctic terns that nested down on the spit.

Everyone knows the small, white, briskly aggressive bird with its black hood, so formidable and forward that many of the larger birds flee from it in a panic.

Arctic and great skua, ravens, and even black-backed gulls take wing when a swarm of terns descends upon them.

The little girl didn't dare risk her life by going down to the spit. If the six-year-old boy had been with her and had held her hand and led her down, then it would have been a different matter. They would have been armoured with old caps and threaded their ponytails through holes in the crown, but this time she had no such luck.

The thing is, the boy had gone fishing in the old, rotting dinghy with the other boys from Ystibær, even though they had been forbidden from doing so on more than one occasion. But warnings mean next to nothing when boys like that are concerned. They do whatever they want.

She stood and shuffled a little, unsure of what to do.

Why do birds behave so peculiarly? Why did these build their nests in this place, but others in a different place altogether?

Why do eagles perch on the highest branches, merlins and falcons on precipices, but the plover prefers the hills and the whimbrel the wetlands?

Why? That was the big question.

The girl paced forward and backward, a little uneasily, to try to get some warmth in her feet.

Then she spotted the great wonder, the plover's nest.

It was right at her toes. Such a marvel. She felt certain it was a plover nest but couldn't say for sure.

It had been left—thoughtlessly so—defenceless in the stony terrain, exposed to the freezing northern wind.

An icy gust blew from the northwest, sweeping over the vulnerable eggs, these four golden-brown eggs dappled with black speckles.

The girl lost her breath. Where were its mamma and pabbi? The eggs can't tolerate this cold.

They would never hatch. They would freeze to death inside their shells in these icy gales.

Something had to be done.

Their mamma and pabbi might be off in search of food, fighting the pangs of hunger.

How could she help?

She couldn't use her damp, poor overshirt; that would only scare away the parents.

But there must be something to do. The wind was biting. The girl double-stepped aimlessly, rubbing her cold palms together. The nest was defenceless, writhing in the gales.

There was only one thing to be done. She needed to build a wall to protect them, and to build it fast. There was no hope the birds themselves could do it, since they didn't have hands.

She started at once—she was already half-numb, but that meant nothing—now it was do or die.

First, she took a few of the largest stones she'd found in the ungiving gravel and arranged them in a half circle to the northwest of the nest. She marvelled at her work for a quick moment, but then she realized, with the eyes of an architect, that this wouldn't be enough. The wall needed to be taller to make a difference.

But her materials were depleting. There was little at hand but a few stones, rounded in all the wrong ways, difficult to stack. Her swollen hands toiled over these cumbersome materials, and, despite the nearly insurmountable difficulty of it, the wall grew little by little.

It now formed a shelter around the nest. The little girl with the numb hands had engineered something great, relative to the skills and size of the builder.

It was a half ring of small boulders and bulky, circular pebbles stacked into a wobbly stone wall with a weak foundation.

It was like the house built on sand.

The little child paused abruptly and looked at the work of her hands with all the victory and pride of an engineer.

Now all was saved. Now these blessed plover young would never be cold, even if the north-western wind lashed them.

She, a little wretch nobody believed could achieve anything, had achieved this. She had helped these poor little birds who did not have hands to build a windbreak themselves.

Surely god could see it. He who watched all seeing from the high heavens, who had an order of angels at his beck and call—just like the people of Ystibær who ordered the boys about when they managed to keep a tight enough rein on them.

Which only happened occasionally. But the angels were hardly to be reined in, though they could be bridled to a certain extent.

That's what gran said.

And gran always told the truth.

Who exactly bridled the angels for god was something of a curiosity to the girl, but as far as she knew, God was never caught out in the rain. And heaven's floor was definitely dry, especially in weather like this.

The lord's rein-pullers were probably some old, burnt-out angels who were only useful for taming angelings.

But one thing was for certain:

God had seen her feat from heaven on high. And something else was just as certain: An entire group of angel children had gathered around her even though she couldn't see them.

The worst part was that her stepbrother and the Ystibær boys weren't here to see what she could really do.

But you can't have everything. She had to be satisfied with the almighty god and those angels who could be bridled.

At least that was something.

She hoped there were enough angels that someone would admire her handiwork—the work of a genius.

She gazed at her achievement in appraisal, first with arrogance and self-satisfaction; but then she became critical, as masters tend to do.

She kneeled in the gravel to tend to her creation, to correct small weaknesses she'd noticed, and to put the final touches on her masterpiece.

It needed stones on either end to give it the right shape, and its back needed to be reinforced somewhat to withstand the assault of northerly storms.

The girl was now completely numb, but the numbness drained neither her strength nor her resolve.

These young wouldn't perish from the gails and the cold. She had seen to that.

She had now perfected her masterpiece, and put her whole self into it.

All the naughty angel boys whirled around her in a circle, tilting their heads and marvelling at her and her creation. Its like had never been seen in these parts; there had never been so much as a cairn here.

Now, there was only one thing left to do: To set two large stones slightly above it to mark this wonderful phenomenon so that she could cut a path straight to it next time.

What a glory it will be, when the young hatch from their eggs, their little beaks break through their shells, tweeting as they emerge.

She forgot about her cold, wet clothes, her little frozen hands, and the wind whipping from the north. She stepped in place in gleeful excitement.

She bent down and adjusted the most beautiful stone in the windbreak.

Then, a horrible accident.

It all tumbled down; this child's masterpiece crashed like a landslide onto the fragile, russet eggs with their tiny black speckles.

She didn't cry in that first moment. She lowered down to her knees, steadied herself with her numb hands, and lost her breath for a speechless second.

Then came the tears, the violent tears of a child in a frenzy over the blind horror of brutal death.

What had happened?

The destruction before her tear-filled eyes was irreversible, irreplaceable, irreparable.

There was nothing to be rescued.

The child cried with fury, and all the naughty angel children began to shriek, too, even though nobody could hear them but the girl. She listened to their painful despairing cries with the sensitive ears of a child.

Now, everything was razed—all destroyed—all the little young were dead because their eggs had been crushed, leaving only a gross gallimaufry.

The child stayed frozen and bawled. It was the desperate cry of one who knows that all is lost—their work ruined, their hope exhausted—all is over.

Finally, when the violent sobs stilled, a clear, calm idea came to her:

The plover mamma and pabbi must never see.

The dark pearls of their eyes must never behold the sight of their children's horrible deaths.

What could she do? She sniffled, shifting her weight from foot to foot as she tried to gather her thoughts. Despair crippled her mind for a moment; her judgement had gone out the window.

She was still kneeling in the rough, glaring-wet stones.

Then a solution came to her from the omnipresent, magnanimous god in heaven on high.

The naughty angels, who were never tamed because they were so defiant and determined, stooped snivelling next to this child of the earth, and tried to assist her to the best of their divine ability.

It exceeded all expectations. The girl dug in the gravel with her small, weak fingers.

She filled her little palms with coarse stones and eggy ooze, which clung to her bruised and bloody hands like glue. She had no other vessel than her little powerless palms. She was ferrying the shattered eggs down to the bog.

She was going to sink the remains in the water.

She felt the angels circling around here, trying with all their might to help her. It exceeded all expectations.

It was quite a wonder how her little hands held onto to the rubble and the slime, and how much they could bear.

Blood trickled from her purple, powerless fingers but the child dried them every so often on her red trousers. She didn't dare dirty her torn and tattered coat more that she already had.

After a long and difficult time, the whole mess was sunken in the bottom of the bog.

The child stood on the hill. She'd stopped crying, and her whimpers had faded for the most part.

Now, there was only one thing left to do: To level her masterpiece.

She crouched down. Her knees were swollen and bloody, but she didn't feel it.

She picked up the wall's remaining stones and tossed them as far as she could, one by one, all around.

Nothing less would soothe the child's troubled mind.

The tears dried on her puffy face. She blew her nose into her hands, and then wiped her hands and face with moss. Now, it was even with the earth. Nobody could see that anything at all had taken place there.

The child still had to take the heaviest step.

She needed to remove the two large stones meant to guide her way to the adorable plover nest so that she could find it without any trouble.

The girl lifted the big stones one after another. She threw them as far as she could, with a strength inconceivable for how exhausted she was.

It was the grit and endurance of the hopeless, of the destitute.

She strode home, heavy-hearted, through the marsh.

Because it was over.

She trudged through black ooze up to her knees and the angels waded after her—they were so mournful and downcast that they had fallen out of flight.

Their little wings, some more clean than others, though they all ought to be called white, were folded on their backs as if they were pinioned in place. This pained procession waded through the rust red marsh and ashen clouds of midges on the journey home.

None cried aloud any longer, but they all sniffled, swollen with cold, crusted with blood, vanquished.

In the distance, the restless, searching, pleading *pipi—the glory, the glory*—of grief-stricken parents who have lost everything; their home, their children, the glory of spring—all of it gone fully and completely.

IN WHICH PRAM

Some people are quick to heap abuses on you, even when you haven't done a thing to deserve it—you've merely observed their prams and tried to take a peek inside a one or two, quick as you can.

They seem to find it strange that you'd be wont to poke around in things that are none of your concern.

And it's true. It really is none of your concern, since you've never even owned a pram and no longer have a child, either.

But that doesn't make any difference. You can't resist the urge to see what's in the carriages all around you, regardless of what their owners may think or do. And maybe that does concern you a little bit.

It's astonishing how unique they all are, even though they come in droves. You see their differences most clearly when you tiptoe around them and admire their dressings; when you listen to each subtle sound with pricked up ears, like a little boy examining the cogs of a clock.

Some are strikingly beautiful, with adorable colors—the canopy is sewn from gabardine the color of red lilac blossoms, and the carrycot itself is slick, lacquered. You can see your reflection in its bassinet. Its white rubber wheels are so soft they spin without making a sound. And the footbrake between them responds to the lightest tap; it stops the pram gently, even on a slope. The wheels are so large that you hardly have to lean forward to glimpse the baby.

There it coos, wrapped in a warm down blanket like a hatchling in a nest, its little face peeking out from between soft lace pillows like mounds of snow, its eyes filled with wonder.

A pristine baby bottle with notches along the side and a fashionable nipple are raked into a corner. When you catch the faintest whiff of baby powder and milk, your heart hammers.

Still, this child is a stranger to you.

Fine prams are immaculate works of art. Everything is in its place: pristine diapers folded at baby's feet and a little, lovely rattle dangling from the shade. Everything is decided in advance: each object fits with another to form a harmonious whole—everything is in order, the child and the pram.

– Gosh, how you envy that woman!

But there are ugly prams, too. They're awkward to maneuver; of necessity, they're botched together out of random parts, out of whatever materials were immediately at hand.

A basket that was originally intended for the washing is rigged to a scooter or roller skates. The workmanship is shoddy. The pronged skeleton of a beat-up umbrella, its fabric replaced with a shabby waxcloth from the kitchen table, is patchworked over the bassinet in place of a canopy. And everything is painted black with shoe polish.

You nearly double over to see the baby inside because the wheels are so low to the ground. Its bedclothes are gaudy calico, the pillowcases cut from a different cloth. Yet the baby's head rests on a pillow—a delightful baby, surrounded by shambles.

Its milk is kept in an old medicine bottle. The label has been partially scratched off, revealing to any passerby that its contents have curdled.

A few packages are placed near the baby's feet—among them, a rust brown paper bag on its side that a few potatoes have rolled out of.

A subtle sour smell wafts from the pram and sometimes a pleasant, sweet-acrid odour, too, when the child inside has wet itself.

You get butterflies in your fingers, but dare not touch anything—instead, the only option is to bend down and hope that nobody catches you.

But it's all the same whether a pram is attractive or ugly—at the worst moment, the mother will inevitably come running with suspicion in her eyes and tout something under her breath. And you'll scamper off, shame running down your face and a stab in your heart out of envy for this woman!

But this baby doesn't concern you. You're doing something that isn't allowed.

And so, the women push their prams away and all that's left to do is watch them from a growing distance, tightening your fist, holding your breath.

The posh ones flip the brake with their toes and the pram rolls forward, soft and noiseless, like a magic carpet in a fairy tale.

How sweetly the child must be dreaming!

Mothers smile absentmindedly at the sky, and fathers jog at their sides and help them steer when the pram rolls down a slope or they struggle to push it uphill. Their peaceful and calm faces betray how pleased they are with themselves for thinking of everything in advance. The lady knows what she's going to buy and where she's going to shop and how much money will be left after; and while she steps into the store, the husband waits outside with the baby even though the brake is locked, and the pram isn't going anywhere.

And he raises his hand to the brim of his hat if he encounters acquaintances. If their wives are with them, he tips his hat using his thumb and forefinger. It's a smart and stylish gesture, a civilized greeting and it secretly makes him feel big and important.

They take on the same expression of students roaming the streets in graduation caps for the first time, trying to make as if it's nothing much, nothing remarkable.

But the wives of these acquaintances shoot this dad teasing, even flirtatious glances, then look into the pram without the least shyness, and say something absolutely inane to the kid:

– Wook 'ow pwetty, wittle wove! Or something similarly intelligent.

And you begin to feel sore about it, and your blood rushes to your head from excitement because you yourself want to look under the tiny canopy and say the same.

But you can't make yourself do it. They're so fine and ladylike, and you're nothing but a wretch, a silly girl with a bare head, wearing the wrong clothes.

No. You have to sate yourself on stealing and sneaking, like an amateur thief crouching at a locked safe. And even when you've only managed to see the tip of its nose as you hurry past – yes, even then you can be content that it wasn't your baby, since your baby doesn't have such a nose.

It really is better to deal with an ugly pram. The women who push them are most often alone, and a throng never gathers around them to poke at the baby.

But it must be an ordeal to go into town with this sort of pram because people gape so at the tired, rawboned woman pushing it, and they contort their faces into a curious expression, an ambiguous puckering at the corners of their mouths.

But the child needs fresh air, just like the children in real prams, and the woman needs to do the shopping—alone. If she were engaged or married, her boyfriend wouldn't want to stand outside with the pram, even if she just needed to pop into the store to ask what something costs.

And her friends wouldn't want to help her push and wouldn't want to walk with her but for a moment because of the state of the pram. But someone still has to keep an eye on such a carriage when you steal away so that it doesn't roll off or the child doesn't tumble out. Anything could happen. Most often, there aren't any brakes on

these prams and if they're on a scooter or skates, they're unsturdy.

I imagine you remember being on skates yourself not that long ago. Once you've kicked off, it's near impossible to stop, and you don't really have any say in what direction you'll go; they can whisk you out into the street just as a car barrels toward you, and you can't swerve out of the way or stop on your own, and sometimes you fall right in front of the car and the driver slams the brakes and the tires burn the asphalt, and they tell you off. They might even give you a whopping. But you still did it over and over; you couldn't stop yourself because it was so fun, so thrilling to be unable to stop yourself at the most urgent moment.

The nature of roller-skates doesn't change just because you stick a basket on top of them and call it a baby carriage.

These carriages occasionally drag women behind them all the way down the slope of Bankastræti. They're forced to run after them, breathless and bursting with frustration, until the roller-skates are eventually brought to a halt by a pothole. They fix their prams to a handrail near the steps and don't dare wander off until they've stuck a stone behind the wheels, even though the pram is on even ground.

They mop their brow with the back of their hand and calculate whether they have enough to buy meat for dinner. In the meantime, you lie in wait, aim for the pram like a cat sizing up a mouse, pouncing only after the woman has gone into the store.

Even though you've never owned a pram yourself, it's impossible not to notice these things when you circle these carriages and sneak a peek inside them while the mothers are away. You're careful not to touch the ugly carriages; they might roll away and something bad could happen.

A stone isn't always at hand to brace the wheel.

The babies in Silver Cross prams cry at times, just like those in the other ones, and that gives you a good and valid reason to peek under the canopy and babble sweet words to the baby, even when their dads are right there. Fathers mean well but are, without fail, inept at comforting babies. And nobody could blame you for wanting to comfort a child that's crying, regardless of whether you're a chit of a girl or a fine lady.

If you're comforting a child in a Silver Cross, or any real carriage, then you shake its rattle and make a funny face. But if it's in the other type, you make clucking noises and wiggle your fingers because there is no rattle.

If nobody is nearby, you reach for the bottle and ease the nipple into the baby's mouth, but if the parents are close, you don't dare. It's presumptuous to give someone else's child a bottle.

When mothers catch you red-handed, all you can do is hurry away and look with reverent adoration at the child.

Women with ugly prams turn still bluer in the face; some of them look like they've been found out. They yank their young away in their jalopies, which jangle and shake. The precarious carriages drag them along; they try to dig their heels into the curbstone, but they're as helpless as a dory boat dragged by a barge.

The fine ladies peer at you out the corners of their eyes with a sort of benevolent scorn and inspect the baby to make sure you haven't ruined it. Then they swish away like yachts in a favorable wind, and send you a feigned saintly smile.

And you try to beat it into your own head that you don't have a child anymore – since this one isn't a black-haired boy, but a little blonde girl, whose hair, eyes, and mouth are completely unlike his. And it certainly doesn't concern you. This is the child of another woman. But it still hurts. You still clutch your hands behind your back to stop yourself from snatching her and never letting her go – it certainly does concern you – oh yes!

Maybe you really didn't have a child?

No. You gave birth, you writhed and screamed in pain like a wild animal in a wildfire – and you nearly died, though you heard the distant voice of a doctor say:

– It's a boy, miss.

And in a haze as if in a dream, you felt a little warm bundle in the crook of your arm. Maybe you only dreamed up those pearlescent blue eyes and those black curls beside you?

Maybe you only dreamed your breasts were bursting, that you were bursting to let him suckle? Maybe. Because the next morning he was gone and your milk had seeped into your clothes and stiffened like blood. But you didn't only dream it when you cried and searched and prayed to god that this unknown woman would return him, bring him back to his mother, who loved him so much because you were, after all, his mother—it makes no difference that you were just a promiscuous girl and he was just an American soldier and you just couldn't stop, no more than you could in the old days, but you're a mother, still, you're the mother of this boy.

Neither is it a dream when you hope and pray that god lets him be in one of these carriages, that god lets you find

179

him, lets the little boy recognize his mother and smile at her.

No, it's not just idle curiosity when you look in every carriage. Because it does concern you, it concerns you deeply, no matter what anyone says. Maybe you no longer have your boy, but nobody can stop you from loving him and searching for him.

You hope he's in one of the proper ones, but that's by no means certain; you have to look everywhere because this wonderful baby boy with those pearl blue eyes, that dimple in his left cheek, those obsidian curls is in one of them, but in which pram?

Acknowledgements

It is my sincere hope that I have approached these texts with the humility and precision of a true craftsman, and that they hold, but do not restrain, the trembling energy that galvanized them. I would like to thank the following people, without whom this work would not have taken shape or shaped me:

Duncan Lewis, the patient editor-in-chief of Nordisk Books, who took a chance on her;

Gunnhildur Jónatansdóttir, who carefully critiqued each translation, offering up thoughtful direction for re-encoding Ásta's Icelandic in my English;

Ásta's children and estate for their generousness and warmth;

My sister, Windy, for her unwavering support;

Haukur Ingvarsson, who helped me to understand where Ásta came from;

Reykjavík UNESCO City of Literature and The Writers' Union of Iceland, who supported my travels to the Bread Loaf School of English, where my cohort read these texts critically and creatively;

Yvette Siegert, who revealed to me sirens, and encouraged me to follow them;

Lucie Brock-Broido, who believed in visitation and the power of the leap;

Sjón, who brought Ásta back into the spotlight, and who has always advocated for voices on the edge.

I thank all the contributors to Ástusögur and The History of Icelandic Literature and all past and present scholars of her life and work.

And thank you, Ásta.

Also by Nordisk Books

Havoc
Tom Kristensen

*You can't betray your best friend
and learn to sing at the same time*
Kim Hiorthøy

Love/War
Ebba Witt-Brattström

Zero
Gine Cornelia Pedersen

Termin
Henrik Nor-Hansen

Transfer Window
Maria Gerhardt